MW00769719

"This book has all the compelling story to unforgettable. You'll l reading."

Sarah Reinhard, author,
SnoringScholar.com and
A Catholic Mother's Companion to Pregnancy

"This captivating murder mystery made me laugh, cry, and crave Italian food; '80s pop tunes are still stuck in my head. If you like mysteries that offer a good mix of suspense and science, don't miss this book."

Barb Szyszkiewicz, *franciscanmom.com*

"Don't You Forget About Me...is a rollicking fun and exciting cozy murder mystery. The author's strong and clever command of the written language makes this book an entertaining page-turner. I recommend this highly-enjoyable, cozy, clean, lively mystery to all readers!"

Therese Heckenkamp,
award-winning author, *Frozen Footprints*

"A quirky, fun, mystery-romance that will tickle your funny bone while making your hair stand on end."

AnnMarie Creedon,
best-selling author, *Angela's Song*

"The book has all the elements of a good novel, with its principal charm resting in Erin McCole Cupp's affable and believable characters. I read (it) in a single sitting, and then put the book down with the wistful feeling of someone departing a gathering of friends."

Celeste Behe, blogger at *A Perpetual Jubilee*,
(celestebehe.blogspot.com)

"It's easy to identify and sympathize with protagonist Cate Whelihan as she returns to her hometown and faces not only the classmates who bullied her in school but also her junior high sweetheart and fellow nerd, Gene. Readers will be chuckling one moment...and biting nails the next as she faces threats, corrupt police, and the business end of a gun."

Daria Sockey, author,
*The Everyday Catholic's Guide
to the Liturgy of the Hours*

DON'T YOU FORGET ABOUT ME

A Novel

ERIN McCOLE CUPP

Beth,
Good to see you!
Veritas!
Erin

Full Quiver Publishing
Pakenham, Ontario

This book is a work of fiction. The names, characters and incidents are products of the author's imagination. Any similarity to actual events or persons living or dead is purely coincidental.

Don't You Forget About Me
copyright 2013 Erin McCole Cupp
Published by Full Quiver Publishing
PO Box 244
Pakenham ON K0A2X0
Canada

Cover design by James Hrkach
Cover Photography by Scott Cupp
ISBN Number: 978-0-9879153-3-7
Printed and bound in USA

NATIONAL LIBRARY OF CANADA CATALOGUING IN PUBLICATION

Scripture texts in this work are taken from the *New American Bible, revised edition* © 2010, 1991, 1986, 1970 Confraternity of Christian Doctrine, Washington, D.C. and are used by permission of the copyright owner. All Rights Reserved. No part of the New American Bible may be reproduced in any form without permission in writing from the copyright owner.

ALL RIGHTS RESERVED
No part of this publication may be reproduced, stored in a retrieval system or transmitted, in any form or by any means - electronic, mechanical, photocopying, recording or otherwise - without prior written permission from the author.

Copyright 2013 Erin McCole Cupp
Published by Full Quiver Publishing
A Division of Innate Productions

With gratitude
to Dr. Mark F. Stegman, M. D.
and all the dedicated health professionals
at Holy Spirit Hospital
for providing healing, hope and truth

1986

LIFE IN A NORTHERN TOWN

The angle of the sunlight cries "late afternoon." The quiet suggests a Saturday. A concrete railway bridge arches over a valley etched by a creek. A train bound for Philadelphia thunders across the bridge's tracks. The sounds of the train's insistent, mournful horn and its clamoring wheels fade off into the distance. The smell of decaying leaves and something faintly chemical laces the air.

The creek's course is clogged with autumn leaves. The bridge is afflicted with only a thin smattering of graffiti at the ankles of its arches, because nobody—hardly anybody—ever comes this deep into the park. This is a rare time, though. Two boys are marching down the slope. Their brightly laced high-top sneakers slog through the leafmeal. Their limbs are gangly. Their Adam's apples already protrude. If you look carefully enough, you can see that one of them has started shaving. The other, the one with the slightly golden tone to his brown hair, has a soft down on his upper lip, signaling the approach of that milestone.

"So whatcha find down here?"

"You'll see." The shorter, darker boy with the stubbled lip has a backpack slung across one shoulder.

"Better be something good if you're dragging me all the way down here," says the boy with the lighter hair.

The boy with the darker hair swallows, his Adam's apple bobbing. "Yeah. Something you've never seen before."

"Better be." This boy sniffles, then wipes his nose with

the bottom hem of his powder blue "CYO 7-8 BASKETBALL" jersey.

The darker boy is breathing heavily. Balancing his backpack, he skids down the slick leaves a few yards, catching himself on one of the boulders sticking out of the slope. "Hey, aren't you hungry?"

"Starving. You got food?"

"My mom made cookies. You want one?"

"What kind?"

"Amaretti."

"What for? It's not Christmas."

The boy with the backpack freezes for a second, his wide brown eyes even wider. He recovers. "I dunno. She likes to cook, I guess."

"I'll tell you what else she likes," *cracks his friend.*

The darker haired boy spits out a curse learned from his Sicilian grandmother and unzips his backpack. "You want a cookie, you're gonna shut up about my mom."

For a second, his friend makes his face solemn, but it doesn't last. He's laughing again, but he gets his cookies anyway. "Don't you want any?"

"Not hungry. Come on, Tony. Eat and walk."

The golden boy reaches into the white paper bag and shoves one cookie, then another, into his mouth as both boys walk with sideways feet down the steepness of this hill. The boy with the backpack leads the way, looking back at his cookie-eating friend at every step.

"What are you looking at?"

"Nothing. We're almost there."

He leads Tony across the leaf-slicked rocks that line the bank.

"Is it in the creek?"

"Yeah. It will be."

The leader lights on one rock, then another, and then

he is standing above the creek's slowly moving waters. He looks back one more time and sees Tony standing on the rock he himself had just left. Tony is coughing. Tony is grasping at his throat. Tony is looking helplessly at his friend one rock away.

Tony's friend sobs, the tender sob of a boy trying very hard to become a man. "I'm sorry, Tony. I had to. I'm really, really sorry."

Tony falls. The other boy freezes there, staring while Tony's body shudders, seizes, then grows still. The other boy blinks repeatedly then runs across the creek. Minutes later, he has disappeared up the opposite slope, leaving his friend face-down in the creek's babbling waters.

A few hours later, a lone, redheaded teenage girl will walk up this creek. Her life will be changed, too.

2012

CHAPTER ONE
WANNA BE STARTIN' SOMETHIN'

"You're going."

I stuck out my lower lip and sighed in that way that makes my curly red bangs flutter over my eyes. "I'm sending a fruit basket to the convent."

"As your agent, Cate, I insist. You're going."

"As your client, Becky, I tell you that I'm making a donation to the school and sending a thoughtful note through your office. I don't want them to have my real address."

Staz yelled from the living room, "You're going!"

"Is that Staz?" Becky asked.

"You can't make me go." I pointed my phone at Staz's bulbous belly. "Geoff won't let you. You're going to pop any minute."

"You told me she's not due until next month," Becky scoffed back, loudly enough that I could hear her even before my phone was back at my ear.

Staz wagged her finger at me from her place on her couch. "You're going."

"And that's final," Becky added in my ear.

At least Staz was around to see me roll my eyes. "Give me one good reason why I should go."

"Sure," Becky said. "I'm good with fish in a barrel. First, it's great PR. Local girl makes good, becomes award-winning children's author, and returns to honor the memory of her grade school principal—a sweet old nun, might I add—who helped her reach the pinnacle upon which she sits today."

"First," I said, "I can see why you're an agent, not an editor. That's way too long for a headline. Secondly, everybody hates nuns, and Sister Thomas Marie was anything but sweet."

Staz was mumbling something about more butter cookies. I turned to find her rocking back and forth on her hips, building up enough momentum to launch off the couch and into the kitchen. Phone still at my ear, I went over to her and gave her my arm. We both grunted as she made it to her feet.

"I don't hate nuns," Staz said, "and I'm Jewish."

Becky continued. "Secondly, I'll appeal to your usually generous heart. Maybe there's some little girl at St. Bumblebutt Elementary—"

I pressed my spare hand to my forehead. "Our Lady of the Seven Dolors."

"—who dreams of being a writer, but she lives in Podunk, Pennsylvania, where dreams go to die."

I heard a metallic *thunk*, followed by, "Oy!" I found Staz in the kitchen, glaring down at the floor as if betrayed. The butter cookie tin had fallen. Staz grabbed the counter with one hand and made to squat and pick up the tin. I ran after her, swatted her shoulder and pulled her back up to standing. Then I handed her the cookie tin off the floor.

"*Grazie*," she said, breathless.

All the while, Becky nattered on in my phone. "But if Mary Cate Wheeler, world-famous author of the Alexander McSomething series, came to Saint Dodo's school with an inspiring message of—"

"Becky, I am happy to do school visits—"

"I win!"

"—anywhere but Seven Dolors."

Becky grunted. "Well then, Miss I-don't-have-time-for-social media, don't you at least want to catch up with your old classmates?"

I cracked up. "Hey, Staz. Becky thinks I might want to

catch up with my grade school classmates."

"I want you to go rub their noses in it," Staz said around her second butter cookie.

Staz is loud enough by nature that Becky could hear her through the phone. "There!" Becky said, sounding quite confident of her triumph. "If you're not into do-gooding, what about delicious vengeance? Cold? Sweet? Even better than ice cream?"

I sighed again, leaning against Staz's counter, looking up at the skylight. "Clearly you are not familiar with Walkerville's culture."

Staz snorted next to me. "Or lack thereof."

I took a butter cookie from the tin. Staz whimpered and yanked the box out of my reach.

"I dare you to run away with that," I murmured out of the phone.

"What?" Becky asked.

"Not you. Staz. Anyway, I'm not going."

"She's going!" Staz said through a fine shower of cookie crumbs.

"Am not."

Becky was silent. For a split second, I thought I had won. Then she struck the worst blow. "Well, it seems at least one of your former classmates is a fan of yours."

"You mean one of their kids is."

"Mmm-nnn." I heard Becky clacking at her keyboard. "No, the media relations department forwarded me this email from your author account, asking if you were coming to Sr. Thomas Marie's funeral this weekend. He says he has read all your books over the years—assuming this was the pen name for Mary Catherine Whelihan—and he was hoping to see you."

"'He?'"

Staz's eyebrows went up. "'He?'"

"Yes," Becky said. "This email is from one Eugene Marcasian."

I felt my cheeks get, well, not hot, but at least lukewarm. "Oh. Gene."

"You might call him Gene," Becky said, "but from his signature line, I bet his patients call him 'Doctor.'"

"Well, knowing Gene, his becoming a doctor is not a surprise."

"'He'?" Staz said. "'Doctor'? Now you're definitely going."

"Victory!" Becky shouted from her end.

"Easy there, ladies." I stuck my palm in Staz's face. "Nobody's going anywhere yet. Gene's probably married by now, like everybody else in the world except me. It's more likely he read the series to his kids, and he just wants an autograph for them."

"So he's married," Becky said. "Maybe he'll need some consoling, and with his wife at home with the rugrats..."

I closed my eyes for a second and remembered the eighth grade retreat. I remembered standing out behind the retreat center dining hall with Gene, the winter air like knives in my nostrils each time I breathed in. I remembered how the light from the kitchen windows made squares on the snow as we stood in the thick shadow between them. I remember reaching for Gene, him reaching for me, and then I remember him pulling away.

"No," I said to Becky. "Gene is not the cheating type."

Staz raised her eyebrows in a question.

"I don't know." Becky clucked at me. "Twenty-five years can change anybody."

"Not Gene," I said. I sighed. Then I felt myself thinking, *At least I hope not.*

"Well," Becky went on, "unlikely as that may be, he did say in his email that he wants to ask you and some of your other classmates a question, but it's very personal, and he's not comfortable asking over email."

"What?" Staz whispered at seeing my expression. "What is it?"

I held my hand up and shook my head, mouthing, *Later*. "Does he say anything else?"

"Nope," Becky said. "Just that he hopes he'll see you at the funeral."

"Well?" Staz asked.

I studied the butter cookie in my free hand and pressed the weight of my phone against my cheek. I felt like I might throw up. It was the same feeling I would get every time I worked myself up to go to a Junior CYO dance— terrified of spending a night immersed in mocking and isolation, but not willing to miss whatever might happen at something as magical as a dance.

Not willing to find out what would happen if Gene went there without me.

"Fine," I said. "Forward the email to my personal addy."

"Good," Becky said, "because I've already booked you a hotel, and your school has an author visit contract on my desk just waiting for you to sign."

"Becky!"

Staz was giggling, holding her burgeoning belly with one hand. "She already has it all set up, doesn't she?"

I glared at Staz in the same way she had just glared at the traitorous cookie tin. Then I thought of Sister Thomas Marie.

"Becky," I said into the phone, sinking onto one of Staz's breakfast nook stools, "can you do me one favor while I pack?"

"Yes, ma'am."

"Can you send some flowers to the church for the funeral?"

"What kind? Roses? Lilies? I realize they're traditional, but to me they always seemed kind of—"

"Poppies," I said. "For Sister Thomas Marie? Send tall poppies."

CHAPTER TWO
GOODY TWO SHOES

Walkerville was about three hours south of the little college town where both Staz and I lived, so I didn't need to leave until the next morning. I stayed at Staz's house and helped her make dinner while we waited for her husband to come home. Geoff would be at the local martial arts school teaching a Krav Maga class until seven.

Staz was already on summer break. Being due in late June, she had decided not to teach any summer classes this year. I usually would have taken this time either to do quick book promotion tours or just work on the next Alexander McSomething story, but I was between books and, what made it worse, was suffering a pretty vicious case of writer's block. It seemed Alex wanted to take a summer break, whether I wanted her to or not.

Yes, Alexander is a she, a time-traveling, computer-hacking, practical joking child genius who was introduced to the world in *Alexander McSomething and the Personality Machine*. She was my graduate thesis project. Much to my surprise, she was my first real success. I'm still waiting for Becky or my editor to call me and say, "Oh, by the way, we finally realized that you're a huge fraud, and the Newberry people want you to scrape off that medal they put on all those copies of *Alexander McSomething and the Defeat of Dustin Dread*."

So it's good that I have Staz and her husband, Geoff, to remind me that Mary Catherine Whelihan is a valuable person, even when she's not Mary Cate Wheeler, Children's Author.

"So," Geoff asked as he poured another glass of water for Staz, "explain to me again why you're going to this funeral?"

Staz, too pregnant to reach across the table to get the pitcher herself, swallowed her mouthful of spaghetti. "To kick some Sicilian butt."

I nearly snorted iced tea out my nose.

Staz added, "Metaphorically speaking."

Anastasia Greenfield Molinsky, PhD, has been my best friend since the first moment of Physics Lab 101 at Korton State University in 1991. I had arrived late, having gotten lost in a rather labyrinthine physical sciences building. There was only one seat left, and it was in the dead front of the room—the last place in the world I would have wanted to sit for a science lab. There was only one other person sitting at that table, and she was a girl whose dark brown hair was even curlier than my red hair. She wore a huge pair of silver-framed John Lennon glasses, an Echo and the Bunnymen t-shirt, a ripped pair of jean shorts, and knee-high Doc Martens.

I sat down next to her in my pale peach polo shirt and Bermuda shorts. She leaned over to me and asked, "You don't like physics, do you?"

She terrified me, but at least I was able to answer her honestly. "Um, no."

"Good," she said. "Physics is for doofi."

In spite of my social anxiety, I snorted back a laugh. "As in, like, the plural of doofus?"

Her eyebrows went up with pleasant surprise. "English major?"

Sheepishly, I shrugged my shoulders. "What gave it away?"

"You know your plurals. Hey, at least you're not a physics major. I mean, physics? That's just stuff banging together," she said, waving at the Newton Balls on the teacher's counter. "Totally predictable. Chemistry is gorgeous. Even bio's got it going on some, but physics?

Ugly. Boring. Where's the mystery? I'm Anastasia, but everyone calls me Staz."

By sophomore year we were roommates. She introduced me to music, and I introduced her to poetry. By senior year we were looking for graduate schools together. While I was being stalked by a psycho-ex, she made me take a self-defense seminar with her at the Jewish Community Center. Three years later, when she married the seminar's instructor, I was the maid of honor. Staz's was the shoulder I cried on the most through that stalking ex from high school, a failed engagement, and then through the following years of my lackluster dating life. In Geoff she gave me the big brother I never had. Now they were going to make me an auntie.

Most of all, Staz had always given me hope in myself when it seemed none were to be found, so that's what she did on the eve of Sr. Thomas Marie's funeral.

"Seriously, Cate," Geoff asked as he slathered butter on another slice of bread. If Staz was eating for two these days, Geoff was eating for three. "Aren't these the people who peed on your book report in fifth grade?"

I squirmed. "Not all of them did."

"Vandalized your 'Save the Mermaids' poster project?"

"It was 'Save the Manatees,' Geoff," Staz said.

Geoff went on. "Crossed out your real last name and wrote 'Where's the Ham' on your essay contest entry?"

"We're not sure if that was my class or the seventh graders."

Geoff started counting them off rapid fire. "Threw your shoes in the snow during gym class? Pushed you into the boy's bathroom at the eighth grade Valentine's dance? Put gum in your hair five times?"

"Seven," I said.

"And pancake syrup in your hair at some sleepover?"

I cringed. "Gina Maldorone's twelfth birthday."

"Staz?" Geoff turned to his wife, his bushy eyebrows lifted to incredulous heights. "How can you let her face these—these—"

"How can I not let her go?" Staz pointed at me with her fork as if it were a laser pointer and I were a diagram of some complex organic molecule. "Sure, they might have let up on her after she was the one who found their dead—"

Staz met my eyes, but I shook my head. I knew I'd have to go there at the funeral, but not yet.

Staz nodded acknowledgement and started over. "Okay. For ninety percent of her grade school career, these people made our Cate feel like a complete gorgon, when she's one of the most intelligent, beautiful creatures in the world. Look at this hair! Look at this skin—like clouds on a sunny day! Look at those blue eyes!"

Geoff snickered. "Not too much, or my hormonal wife might get jealous."

Staz acted like she hadn't heard him. "People would die for those eyes and those curls, and they made her feel like toilet paper? She needs to walk into that funeral, show them how gorgeous and successful she is, and make them feel like the dreck that they are."

"That's not why I'm going," I said quietly into my plate.

"So why are you, then?" Geoff asked.

"There's a boy," Staz answered just before shoving more spaghetti down the hatch.

"A man by now," I said.

"A doctor," Staz added.

Geoff's eyes flew open. "A kid who peed on your homework became a doctor?"

"No!" Staz and I both shouted.

"Gene was another outcast," I said, "like me."

Staz turned to Geoff. "They were the only two kids in

the class who weren't related to each other—or the mafia."

"Seriously?" Geoff asked.

I shrugged as I poked at my own plate. "Most of my classmates were second generation Sicilians. Stereotypes have to start somewhere."

Staz explained, "It was kind of like growing up on *Jersey Shore*, only Cate was from *The Big Bang Theory*."

I pointed my own fork at Staz. "You're the scientist."

"Right. Cate was Laura Ingalls."

"Aw," I said, "you know me so well."

Staz and I clinked glasses.

Geoff sat there looking from his wife, to me, and then back again several times. Finally he shook his head as if flies were buzzing around it. "If you weren't pregnant, Staz, I'd be going for a beer right now."

Geoff is a sweet guy. He was sticking to all the expectant mom rules in solidarity with Staz. I wondered for a moment if Gene Marcasian were the type to not drink while his wife was pregnant.

"Anyway," I said, "I want to go because Sister Thomas Marie was an influence on me, albeit in that unforgiving, name-your-son-Sue way. Still, she did me good, as much as I hate to admit it. I owe her respect. And if I have to waddle my fat butt—"

"You are not fat," Staz said.

"—through a swarm of skinny, happily married Italian-Americans to do it, then that's what I have to do."

Staz gave me a pointed look. "And then afterwards, Dr. Gene has some personal questions to ask you."

"And our other classmates," I added quickly. "I told you, don't get too excited. Like I said, I'll go to the viewing, say a few polite hellos, answer whatever question Gene wants to ask, then the next morning I'll watch them put Sister in the ground. I'll be back by Thursday afternoon at the latest."

"Oh!" Staz said, "Then you'd better remember your pills. I'm too bulbous to drive them to you three hours away like the last time you forgot them."

I nodded. "Thank you."

"Yeah," Geoff said, "You don't want to run into your outcast doctor friend without your birth control."

"That's not why I take them," I said.

"But treating one's endometriosis does make one a little more prepared for those, you know," Staz teased, "impulsive moments."

I shook my head. "A one-night stand after a nun's viewing? Not bloody likely. Gene and his family were pretty religious when we were kids. I'd put down a twenty that he still is, too."

Staz made a dismissive sound through her teeth. "I'm sure he's outgrown all that by now. You did."

Geoff shrugged. "She's been pretty chaste lately."

Staz tried elbowing him, but he dodged it. Staz lost her balance and nearly fell off the chair. Geoff caught her, and both rippled into a fit of laughter, her alto harmonizing perfectly with his baritone. I couldn't help smiling, even if it were at my expense, and even if they made a duet that I'd pretty much given up hope of ever finding for myself. Their joy at catching each other made me joyful.

"Ugh," Staz said when she'd recovered enough to speak. She pushed her plate away. "Heartburn. I can't eat another bite."

Geoff picked up her plate and went about finishing it for her. I wondered if Gene Marcasian had finished anybody's spaghetti in the past twenty-five years.

CHAPTER THREE
SMALL TOWN

By ten o'clock the next morning, I was packed and in my 1992 white Ford Tempo, on my way south to Walkerville. I had to coax my old car over the Poconos, where there are more candle shops than radio stations, so I plugged my MP3 player into its little portable speakers. I just put it on shuffle and a bizarre mix of Too Much Joy, Adele and Brandenburg Concertos got me through the tunnels and down the northeast extension of the turnpike.

I had not taken this trip in a long time. My parents had moved to Florida years before, so I no longer had much use for driving to my hometown in the northwestern suburbs of Philadelphia. I hadn't even been to Philly in years for anything but book signings. If I were looking for culture, these days I went to New York City just because it was closer. Their cheesesteaks and tomato pie still didn't do it for me, but I wasn't about to take a haul over the Poconos just for greasy junk food.

Sure, I still kept in touch with a few high school friends from track and the literary magazine, but as they got married and had kids, we just drifted apart. I did not drive three hours south to visit them. And, as already established, I did not have any grade school friends who would have enticed me back to Walkerville.

So when I finally pulled into town, I was surprised. Wait. Let me back up. Even before leaving, I had been surprised to see that Becky had set me up in an actual chain hotel. There had been no such animal when I lived there. There had been pretty much nothing but empty storefronts, full bars, pizza shops, and the recently defunct Walker Chemical plant, the carcass of which had dominated the crest of the highest hill in town.

Now there were not one but two real live, actual chain hotels in Walkerville. I parked my car in the lot and looked down the slope at the end of the parking lot, down into Quaker Creek Park. At one time, the park had just been a warren of dark trees, sled-to-your-death hills, and a rusty swing set with no actual swings. Cooler kids than I would go down there to spray graffiti on Walker Chemical's retaining walls and indulge in substances to which I knew to "just say no." Gene and I, however, would meet there in daylight to collect water striders in jam jars, scrape water pennies from under mud-rusted rocks, and scoop crayfish into nets before taking them home to his fish tank. We often walked past the official borders of the park, following the creek in search of what our young minds considered adventure: a rusted bike sloshed along the bank, a fallen log that made a foot bridge.

Then came that evening in the fall of eighth grade. I'd cut across the creek by myself and found something of an adventure that nobody in my class, not even Gene, ever would have wanted.

This day I looked down into a trim valley. A smattering of lunch break joggers ran its paved paths. Children played noisily on a colorful resin play structure, while their mothers observed from cast iron picnic benches. The retaining wall graffiti had been covered over with murals of zoo animals. Not too far away, I heard a whistle and the screech of brakes as a commuter train pulled into Walkerville station, probably the same train my high school friends and I used to take into Philadelphia.

But it was starting to seem like the only thing that hadn't changed was the train to Philly. I pulled my phone from my pocket and texted Staz. *Toto? I don't think we're in Walkerville anymore.*

I got my bags from the trunk and headed into the lobby,

looking over my shoulders for familiar faces. None. My phone buzzed with Staz's reply: *Get your vengeance on. Then click your heels and come home.*

After I checked in and found my room, I picked up the guest directory from the room's little desk. "Shopping" was listed first, and the brand names of some of the boutiques made my eyes bug out: Lily Pulizter? White House Black Market? I muttered something under my breath that a better Catholic than I would have had to mention at confession. Under "Attractions" were listed two art galleries, a playhouse, and a dance club, with a comedy club in the bar of the other new hotel across the creek valley. "Dining" listed three of the five pizza shops I remembered, but now they also had two coffee shops, a wine bar, a vegetarian Indian buffet, and...

I hit caps lock and texted Staz. *THERE'S AN IRISH PUB IN WALKERVILLE?!?!?!?*

How did La Cosa Nostra let a place called Pub Mo Thóin open up in their town? It was like someone had hollowed out the Walkerville where I had grown up, bleached it, and then filled it with diamonds and pearls. And Guinness.

My phone buzzed again. Staz. *Go there. Drink beer. And stop yelling at me.*

"The beer thought's occurring to me," I said out loud.

Phone still in hand, I looked at my laptop case, lying where I had placed it on the desk. I could have stolen time from my toilette and done some writing, but for the first time in my life, the blankness of the laptop screen was even more daunting than my own as-is face in the mirror.

I threw my phone onto the bed and headed to the bathroom to freshen up. And by "freshen up," I mean put in my contacts, smear on as much age-defying and acne-scar-covering makeup as I could, and make liberal use of

my hair straightening iron. I was heading into enemy
territory.

***

It was late May, so the sun was still out when I made
my way across the parking lot back to my car. The heels of
my best pumps, the cute strappy ones that show off my
ankles, clicked across the asphalt in that way that always
made me feel like a grown-up. My light blue blouse dipped
low enough to show the string of pearls I had gotten myself
for my thirtieth birthday, but not so low that I couldn't
walk in to Seven Dolors Church without covering up. I
wore my knee-length black wool skirt. My hair settled well
past my shoulder blades now that it was straightened. A
breeze tickled by me, and I caught a whiff of my own
rosewater perfume. I had treated myself to all those
sensory things that made me feel like I could kick
somebody's butt if need be. Plus, all this was a far cry from
the plaid jumpers I had worn at Seven Dolors. I unlocked
my car, took a bracing breath, then, heart pounding, got in.

Quarter of seven. The viewing had started at six-thirty
and was scheduled to run until nine, but I didn't want to
show up early and sit around by myself. I'd done enough
of that at junior high dances. My plan was to get in the car,
drive around the "downtown" area to make sure what I'd
read in the guest guide hadn't been some kind of joke, then
go to the viewing. My stomach grumbled at how little I
had fed it over the past twenty-four hours, but I was too
anxious to go for an actual dinner. I made a quasi-meal
out of a mini Goldenbergs Peanut Chew I had picked up at
one of the ubiquitous Wawa convenience stores I had
passed on my way down.

But as I drove down the hill to Lower Street, traffic
came to a halt, and I hadn't even reached the side street on
which Seven Dolors was situated. All ahead of me were

brake lights and right turn signals. It looked like I wasn't the only one going to the funeral. My phone dinged with another text from Staz, but, being a good girl for once, I ignored it and craned my neck to see if there were any way around this jam. In moments, a police car pulled up to the next intersection. The officer disembarked, kept his lights flashing, and he began waving people through at appropriate intervals. As my car crawled closer, I saw the officer was none other than Bobby Campobello, Seven Dolors Class of '87.

I gagged down my last bite of Peanut Chew and covered up the stink with a piece of spearmint gum. Bobby was actually one of the last people I would have expected to become a cop. Why? Because of all the troublemaking, bullying boys in my class, he had been one of the nicest. He had even asked me to dance at the party the school held for us after our baccalaureate Mass. You would've thought that one of the shortest boys in the class would've had some sort of Napoleonic issues, but when the second tallest boy in the class is only four inches away, I guess that lessens the urge to make up for lost stature.

My heart bumbled around under my sternum. What should I do? Roll down my window as I passed and say hi? Pull out of traffic and go home? As I got closer, I decided on both fight and flight. I picked up my phone and called Staz.

No answer.

"Crap." I pulled up Becky's number with my thumb. It was after hours. She probably wouldn't be there to—

"Rebecca Ulrich," the phone answered.

"Becky, it's me," I said. "I'm at the funeral. Well, almost."

"Um, good?" she answered, clearly unable to fathom why I was calling her.

Three cars between Bobby and me. Two and a half. "Yeah, there's a lot more—um—traffic heading in than I was expecting."

"Um... less good?"

One and a half more. One. *Please, Lord, don't let him see me. I don't know what to say yet.*

"Cate, are you okay?" Becky sounded legitimately worried. "I'm usually the one calling you. I don't mean to cut you off, but I'm really busy with the new Trini Ross contract. Speaking of which, I didn't get your signed visit contract to fax back to your old school."

That was because I hadn't signed it and had no intention of doing so. "Becky, help me out here," I admitted. "I'm trying to look popular."

"And you're saying it into the phone because?"

"Because the cop knocking on my car window right now is a former classmate. Gotta go."

So much for flight. I rolled down my window and pulled the phone away from my face. "Is there something wrong, officer?"

"Yes, ma'am," Bobby said, not looking at me but instead at the traffic behind us. "No cell phone use while driving in the state of Pennsylvania. Are you here from out of state for the funeral?"

My palms iced on the steering wheel. "Not out of state, exactly, but I am—um—"

Should I let him know who I was? Should I lie? I mean, I was already in a state of mortal sin after having missed Mass and confession for the past, oh, twenty years. What was one more penny in the jar? But before I had to decide, Bobby decided for me.

"Ho-leeeeee—Mary Catherine, is that you?"

I just smiled weakly and shook my head. "I mean, yeah, I'm Mary Catherine, but—"

He pointed to his plastic name badge, reading CAMPOBELLO. "Bobby? Remember me? From your class?"

I felt my cheeks get so hot I was afraid they'd spontaneously combust. "Oh? Ohhhhh! Bobby, right! Good to—"

Behind us, three horns honked in staccato succession. Someone hurled what was probably a Sicilian curse at us. Bobby swatted the air in the curser's direction. His arm dropped very quickly, though, as if it had been manipulated by a puppeteer who had just cut the string.

"Sorry," he said to me, "gotta go, but I'd really like to see you some more. Are you coming to Pub Mo Thóin after the—"

More honking. More cursing.

I grinned and let my voice get all high pitched and nervous. "Don't want to get you in trouble, Bobby. Good to see you!"

My tires squealed around the corner. I guess my first exploration of the new and improved Walkerville would be Sister Thomas Marie's funeral at Our Lady of the Seven Dolors.

***

Wow. It was crowded, far more so than I thought it would be. I followed the slow parade of cars to the parking lot and then past it because the lot was full. I had to drive around for another five blocks on residential streets of gray stone row homes and sidewalks in varying states of repair before I finally found street parking. Cursing the stupid choice to show off my ankles, I found myself hiking up a hill in heels I only wore once or twice a year. Sweat was soaking the back of my neck, not to mention under my blouse. I passed the old brick school building, the attached gym building that my confirmation class had helped finish,

and by the time I made it to the holy water font in the
entry of Seven Dolors, my panty hose were downright
chafing, and only God knew how much of my makeup had
slid off my face in the humidity.

I dipped my index finger into the holy water and
paused. Nope, no lightning or earthquake. I was probably
safe for now. Then I looked around me. It was so heavily
refurbished that this was practically a whole new church.
The old one had caught fire the previous Christmas Eve, a
fact I only knew because my dad had sent me a text
message about it the next day. The steep stone stairs,
which had survived the fire, no longer led directly into the
church but into a spacious vestibule with a high ceiling and
abundant windows.   It looked like the stained glass
windows of St. Anthony (patron of lost stuff) and St.
Therese (pray to her and if you see a rose you'll get your
wish) had survived the blaze.

Throughout this new gathering space, families with
their kids milled about, chatting, their little ones wearing
what was probably the new Seven Dolors uniform: white
polo shirts and khaki skirts or pants. I thought of our old
plaid jumpers and Peter Pan collars. These brats didn't
know how good they had it.

Next to me was a large bulletin board, covered with
flyers and notices. One flyer caught my eye—rather, the
name on it did: The Second Annual "Go for Gloria!"
Family   Softball   Tournament,   benefiting   lifelong
parishioner Gloria Benevento.   I stared stupidly at the
flyer's frame of pink awareness ribbons before the
beneficiary's name clicked in my brain. Gloria Benevento
had been the super-jock girl of our graduating class. She
had been MVP on the CYO basketball team all four years of
middle school, and she had won the state softball pitching
tournament in both seventh and eighth grade.   I

remembered because both years Sister Thomas Marie had a school parade in Gloria's honor. It seemed Gloria was still bringing the Dolors community together, but now for a much graver reason.

I was about to wander over to the line into the church, presumably to pass the casket, when I saw a face I could never forget, no matter how many wrinkles it gained. He had blank hazel eyes, like a hawk in a tree, and a nose that suggested the same bird's beak. Then there was that wide mouth with thin lips and eyebrows that were skimpy but somehow still managed to meet in the middle. It was Arturo DiFranceso. "Turo." Three boys in the new Dolors uniforms stood in front of him, pushing each other. All three were the same height, and all three had the same tank-like shoulders and overall wedge shape as their father had at that age. A woman stood next to Turo. Her hair was brown except for some lighter, gray-streaked roots. Even from a distance I could see that her cheeks were even more deeply acne-scarred than mine, and that's saying something. Slump-shouldered and clothes askew, she looked more than tired. Presumably this was the bully's wife, or at least his babymomma. I felt a wave of pity for her. I turned for another entrance into the nave.

As I slipped into a side entrance, I saw a few more faces I recognized. Maria DellAmoroso was standing with a baby on her hip, and she was talking to Donna Illardo and John Gambino, both otherwise unaccompanied, unadorned with wedding bands. I spied Tina Donato, whose thick mass of curly black hair now seemed tamed into well-conditioned ringlets. Pasquale Marcione was standing next to her, holding her hand. They wore matching wedding bands, too. Hm. There was a couple I hadn't imagined twenty-five years ago. On closer inspection, I noticed that Tina was sporting a baby bump.

Judging from how big Staz had been at that point, I guessed Tina to be about seven months along.

Entering the crowded nave, I expected to smell the crush of sweaty people, or at least the piles of flowers lining the walls and perched all over the sanctuary stair. However, what I smelled was a spicy-sweet tang and freshly baked pillowy crusts, all wafting up from the basement kitchen. That combination was a smell I recognized, a smell that could make even the most Irish of mouths water, even at a nun's funeral. I closed my eyes and inhaled more deeply.

I snuck my phone out of my purse and texted Staz: *Tomato pie.*

As I slid my phone back into my purse, it dinged with another text. People nearby turned and glared at me. Standing near the door, a super-bleach blonde woman approximately my height and age smirked at me through huge glasses so reflective I could barely see her eyes. I felt my cheeks basically set themselves on fire, and I backed out of the nave through the door I was still holding.

Staz. *Is the viewing over already?*

Um...no...

I stayed in the vestibule until I got her reply, six seconds later. *Aren't you supposed to be praying for a dead nun's soul, not sniffing around for tomato pie?*

Don't you judge me! I put my phone on vibrate and headed back into the nave to join the line up to Sister Thomas Marie's casket. I craned my neck around the people in front of me and saw a vase on the floor in front of the St. Joseph statue—a vase full of baby's breath, stattice, pale greenery, and tall red poppies.

Good job, Becky, I thought to myself. I resisted the urge to text her with the compliment.

At the front of the line, directing people which way to

go around the casket, were two ushers. One was a white-haired, stooped old man in a navy blazer, black pants, and scuffed oxblood loafers. I didn't even need to see his face to know it was Mr. Celli, our widower neighbor two doors down when I was growing up, and head usher at Seven Dolors. Still. Wow. It would be true to say he hadn't aged a day since I'd last seen him twenty years ago, but even then he had been old enough to have seen the first fish sprout legs and walk out of the primordial lake.

Honestly, I wasn't all that fond of Mr. Celli, though he'd always been fond of me. Not in a threatening way, mind you, just in that, "You Irish don't eat enough! Here, take these meatballs home. My Nonna would call you a vampire!" way.

There would be no escaping Seven Dolors unnoticed if he recognized me. I was stuck on his side of the line, so I had to pass him. All I could do was hope my straightened hair, plumper figure, and heavy makeup might throw him off the scent. I draped my hair over the one shoulder nearest him and turned to face the casket. And there was Sister Thomas Marie.

I don't know why seeing her dead was such a shock. It's not like I hadn't been given plenty of notice. But it wasn't like looking at the face of my principal, with her gray eyes blazing behind thick-framed glasses, stubs of her steely hair smoothed down by the side of her veil. She was dressed in her black habit and white collar; that much hadn't changed. However, once she had been short and stocky, like a small fortress that walked around in a well-shined pair of black oxfords. Now she looked less dead than deflated. The skin over her cheekbones was no longer puffed out with nutritious convent meals but instead lay like two wet tissues, slathered with cheap foundation and anointed with a hint of blush. The blush stuck out for looking incredibly fake. My stomach turned. I hadn't been expecting her to be this pale.

Her hands were folded on her chest, holding the obligatory set of black rosary beads. They shone with the unyielding glint that her eyes used to have when she swept the Seven Dolors parking lot/recess yard in search of fresh misbehavior. A dainty silver chain twinkled between each Hail Mary and Our Father bead. The crucifix trailed down to her belly, a belly that never bore children on a woman who, in another order, would have been called "mother." And here we who had been her children now filed before her, in a double line, to say our goodbyes. I half-wished she would sit up and tell us to get in size order.

The casket was lined with small mementoes. Holy cards of St. Joseph. Handmade rosaries. Pictures of former students, some in crumbling black-and-white. Had she really been teaching that long? There was even what looked like a report card but in a format I didn't recognize—from a computer printer, not the hand-marked cardstock that got sent home to my parents. Not surprisingly, I saw a picture of Tony Vitale from my class. I wonder which one of us had put it there.

I had expected a reminder of Tony. I had braced myself for the flashbacks. I touched the corner of the photo. In my memory, twenty four young voices prayed, *And may the souls of the faithful departed, through the mercy of God, rest in peace.*

"Amen," I whispered.

Then I pulled my hand back and made ready to move on, but one more memento made me gasp. Without thinking, I reached for it, its petals the color of fresh blood against the pearl silk of the casket linking. I hadn't seen Gene yet. Was he hiding somewhere? If not, who on earth put this tall poppy here?

"*Catarina, bella*!"

I drew in my breath and pulled my hand back. The dull din in the church lowered a bit as some people looked up to see what old Nicolo Celli was shouting about now.

I turned to face my assailant. "Mr. Celli? I almost didn't recognize you!"

He grabbed me by the shoulders and kissed my cheek. His dry lips felt like Sister Thomas Marie's cheeks looked. He must have lost his hearing a bit, because he kept shouting his next words. "Look at you, eh? You finally started to eat!"

There was a soft, collective giggle around us. Fabulous. I dreaded which of my former classmates had heard this and joined in on the laugh. "Yes, Mr. Celli." My cheeks probably matched my hair now. "You got your wish. I've grown both up and out."

He opened his mouth to say more, but the other usher, a twenty-something guy with blond hair and blue eyes—a transplant to Walkerville?—tapped Mr. Celli on the arm and murmured something about keeping the line moving.

"I'll catch you later, Mr. Celli." I gave his arm a quick pat through his polyester sport coat and dashed past him.

I'd just gotten around the corner when Maria, the one with the baby earlier, got up and stood in front of me, saying, "I thought I saw you earlier."

"Maria? Hi," I said. "Good to see you."

She put the arm that wasn't holding her son around me. As I thought, "Dude, why are you of all people hugging me?" I felt my shoulders instinctively stiffen. This was the same person who had, in seventh grade, admitted to me with a sneer that she was the one who had declared, on the gym bathroom mirror in Midnight Wine nail polish no less, that I was something other than heterosexual. Reliving that memory kept me from hugging her back.

I quickly stepped back and said, "He's adorable. Is he your first?"

She smiled, her lips curling back over her long, whitened teeth. "Yeah, finally, after trying for years and years. You cost a fortune, didn't you, sweetie-poo?"

A fortune? I questioned silently as I watched Maria squeeze the little boy's round, rosy cheeks. Strange thing to tell your toddler, but then again declaring another girl's perceived sexual orientation in nail polish isn't exactly a polite form of expression either. I wondered if any of our classmates had changed at all, or did maturity just make us larger, grayer versions of ourselves? If so, what did that make me?

As I opened my mouth to excuse myself, she asked, "Are you going to Pub Mo Thóin afterwards? A bunch of us will be there. I'm gonna drop Timmy here off at my mom's, then—"

"Pub Mo Thóin? I think I read about-—"

"Donna's going to be there, John, all three Franks, Ant and his wife, I even think Bobby's coming, if he's done early enough with this. It's a new place. Gina Maldorone works there."

"Oh, does she? Good for her!" I feigned delight, when really Gina was the only person I had feared more than Turo. She was basically his feminine counterpart in the bully role for our class.

"Do you know where to find Pub Mo Thóin? It's on Lower Street, if you're—"

Okay, it was now my turn to cut her off. "Thanks, Maria. I'll try to stop by."

"That'd be great!" she said, hefting the chubby toddler higher up onto her practically nonexistent hip. "It would be great to catch up. I hear you're some kind of author now or something?"

"Something like that. Nice to see you, and congrats again on your little one."

And with that I headed for the nearest exit. Once back out in the vestibule, out of the corner of my eye, I saw Tina and Pasquale heading in my general direction. I couldn't tell if they'd seen me or not, but as my time back at Seven Dolors progressed, the more I was reminded of how glad I had been to leave and how little I had wanted to come back in the first place.

I ducked into the shadow of an obscenely large floral arrangement, complete with mutant stargazer lilies the size of my head. I made one last visual sweep, looking for Gene Marcasian. When last we'd seen each other, he was already six feet tall. His all-boys Catholic high school uniform had hung off of his skinny frame like a bed sheet drying on a wire hanger, and his newly-applied contact lenses were making him blink nonstop. Over twenty years later, I wasn't even sure what I should be looking for.

As the stink of the lilies soaked into my sinuses, I had to admit that I could not find him. Not tonight, anyway. I had been so uncomfortable at the viewing as well that I now had to ask myself if it was worth hanging around for tomorrow's funeral, hoping to see him, or should I just head back home to face Becky's disappointment and Staz's moral outrage at my cowardice.

Resolving to bravely run away, I stepped out from the overgrown lily garden. In my haste to escape, I accidentally brushed the sender's card out of its plastic fork. I pinched the card up off of the cold stone tiles and slid it back into the holder.

With prayers and sympathies—
Christopher Vitale, CEO
And The Entire Hantzel-Brace-Courton
Pharmaceuticals Family

"Huh. Chris Vitale made it big," I muttered to myself. "Tony must be proud of his big brother."

As I left the weighty perfume of the "pharmaceuticals family" arrangement behind me, another fragrance, far more inviting, readdressed my nostrils. I stopped in my tracks. If I were to be a coward, I would at least be a tomato pie-filled coward. I made a break for the kitchen.

Like I was on some kind of covert mission, I peeked into the church basement. This newly-refurbished hall could only have been Seven Dolors Elementary's café-torium. The room was virtually empty except for the members of the Seven Dolors Ladies' Guild, stomping back and forth between the food tables and the kitchen.

Worried I might be recognized by a former classmate's Nonna, I waited until the coast was clear, tiptoed out to grab a piece of the long-awaited pie, wrapped it in a napkin, and held it in my cupped hands as if it were a baby bird that might fly away. Back on tiptoes so my heels wouldn't clack against the shiny birch flooring, I shuffled to the nearest exit, which placed me out in the back of the building, facing the tree-clad slope down to a branch of Quaker Creek.

Quaker Creek, a ghost from my past. More like a haunted house, only one where a bad thing actually had happened. Regretting my cowardly retreat but not enough to actually go back into the church, I decided I'd face another demon—one not likely to hurt me back. I was going to say my goodbyes to Walkerville by bidding the creek one last farewell. Still holding my tomato pie and hiking my purse higher onto my shoulder, I took a few steps into the woods.

However, within moments my heels sank into the moist earth. I tried to take a step out, but that didn't work out so well. Trying to keep my hands around my tomato pie but still keep my balance on this sharp incline was a move destined for disaster. Before I knew it, my feet slid out from under me, and my arms flew out to my sides to keep me from slipping into the creek entirely. I lost my tomato pie, I lost a shoe, and my favorite black skirt was sliding up my thigh as I skidded down the slope. I flipped onto my belly and dug my hands into the dirt to slow my descent. Finally, I slowed enough to brace myself, each arm caught against a mossy tree trunk.

Cursing profusely, I slowly flipped over onto my back then sat up. I brushed the twigs and dead leaves off of my sky blue blouse only to streak the mud that had been gluing them there. I pulled myself up against one of the trees, kicked off my remaining shoe, and pulled my skirt back down to my knees.

"Did you get my email?"

About ten feet down the slope, holding my unwrapped tomato pie in one palm, in the other a glass jar filled with what could only be creek water, was a tall, sweating, bespectacled Eugene Marcasian, M. D.

CHAPTER FOUR
THERE'LL BE SAD SONGS (TO MAKE YOU CRY)

Tall. Short-clipped hair just starting to gray. Angular. Clearly well-muscled beneath his khakis and rolled-up sleeves. Dark-rimmed glasses over dark hazel eyes. He had actually become so handsome over the past two decades that I just gaped at him for about thirty seconds, my entire abdomen doing the wave in his honor, before I even remembered that I was scratched up, scraped, smeared, disheveled, and, of all things, now shoeless. That kept me stunned for another thirty seconds.

Finally he asked, "Are you okay?"

Stupidly, my hand went first to my hair. My fingers found curls, not straight. Sigh. Even that had fallen apart. "Yeah. I'm just great, thanks."

Gene leaned into the slope and hiked up to me on lean legs. When he reached me, he first rested the jar against the base of a tree, then he looked down at the tomato pie. Holding it out to me, he asked, "Did you want—?"

"No, thanks," I said. "I'll kiss it up to Jesus."

He smiled and tossed the pie over his shoulder. "The squirrels will love it."

I took his hand when he offered it. As he helped me up, I grunted. "Well, at least this saves us that awkward moment of trying to figure out if we should hug or shake hands."

"It does that," he said.

I averted my eyes, but I could feel him looking me up and down as I brushed myself as clean. As lightly as I could, I asked, "Are you checking me out?"

He circled me. "I am."

I nearly fell over at the bluntness. "What?"

He nodded to himself, his dark brows furrowed over his deep-set eyes. "It doesn't look like anything's broken, from the way you're standing. I don't see any major cuts. You do have some abrasions there."

He pointed to my calves, where some minor bleeding was weeping through my decimated panty hose.

I sighed. In relief? Disappointment? Oh, let's not kid ourselves and say it was both. "You're performing first aid," I blurted, sounding a little more annoyed than I should have.

He lifted his eyes back to mine, frowning, maybe a little embarrassed. "Sorry, do I have your permission? I am a doctor."

I snickered uncomfortably. "It's fine, Gene. By the way, it's good to see you, but what are you doing out here and not at the viewing?"

His eyes darted to his creek water jar then back to me. "I could ask you the same thing."

"I just came from the viewing!"

"Into the woods with a snack?"

I felt my cheeks flame up again. "I guess you live near enough you can get real tomato pie any time you want?"

"No," he said, "but I imagine I have been back here more than you have lately."

I raked my hair back over one shoulder and pointed an accusing finger at the jar. "Rounding out your old crayfish collection?"

He bit one side of his lip. "Not exactly, no."

He lunged for one of my shoes and then for the other. As I took them back, I said, "By the way, yes, I did get your email, thank you."

His eyes widened. He pushed his glasses up the bridge of his nose. "So you *are* Marycate Wheeler! With the pen name, I wasn't sure, but when I saw your pictures I was convinced it couldn't be anyone else. I even drove by your parents' old house to ask them, but—"

"Yeah," I said as Gene retrieved his water jar, "they'd moved to Florida right around the time that I started writing Alex."

"Amazing," he said, shaking his head. "I always knew you could do it."

I laughed, out of breath at our ascent. "Do what?"

"Be amazing," he said.

Our feet were back on the asphalt again. Our eyes met. I couldn't think of what to say next. I'm not sure he could either. So I broke the gaze and started paying a great deal of attention to getting my heels back on my battered feet.

"Ow," I said once I was finally re-shoed. "These things hurt when I'm not fresh from a landslide. This is no better."

"Do you need a ride back to your car? I got here too late to park in the lot, but if you wait here, I can—"

"Oh, jeez, Gene, I wasn't fishing for a ride. I'm fine, really, but thank you."

He smiled a little at me—never a smirk. Gene it seemed still wasn't one to smirk. "I take it you're going back in to the viewing then?"

I looked down at my besmirched self. "Well, probably not, to be honest."

"Are you, uh, staying around for the funeral tomorrow?"

He was scratching at the back of his neck with his left hand. As he did so, I saw a thin brown ribbon that had slid out from his undershirt and against his neck. I squinted at it for a second before I recognized it as a scapular cord. Everyone in our class had received one of those at our eighth grade retreat. Sister Thomas Marie had told us to wear them as a symbol of Mary's protection over us. I'd lost mine before I'd even started high school.

But here was Gene, still wearing his. That's also when I

saw what other accessory he wore: the flicker of gold on his ring finger. The panic in my belly whipped up into a fury of disappointment. Just as I suspected. I made a mental note to text an "I told you so" to Staz.

"I'm not sure," I said. "I've said as much goodbye as I came here to say. I guess I was thinking about taking my tomato pie and going home."

"But then you lost the pie," he said.

I grimaced. "But then I lost the pie."

"Does this mean you're staying?"

When I looked back up at Gene, his face was unreadable. He was looking at me with the same detachment as he had when he had looked me over as a potential casualty. He now put his left hand protectively—perhaps with embarrassment—around his jar of creek water.

I admitted, "Well now I have to stay long enough to wash off the blood and dirt, at least."

He laughed a bit. "Good," he said.

"Good that I'm cut and muddy?"

"Good that you're staying," he said.

"Right," I replied. "There's supposed to be some question you had to ask me."

Miraculously, throughout all this my purse had stayed clamped underneath one arm or at least swinging by its strap. I fished in it for my keys and took a few painful steps in the direction of where I had parked.

"There is one question I want to ask several of our classmates," he said as he matched my steps through the parking lot. "But if you're leaving, I guess tonight is my only chance."

"I guess so," I said. I stopped between two rows of parked cars and faced him.

He opened his mouth, then furrowed his brow.

"Actually, I haven't eaten anything since three hours before a c-section this morning, and that was out in Harrisburg. Any chance you're hungry, too?"

The memory of that Peanut Chew in the car was long gone. "Can I get cleaned up first?"

"Of course." He smiled, and his eyes crinkled again. "You owe yourself some tomato pie."

***

I met him an hour later at Bep's Pizza & Grille. Our family used to get its pizza there because, well, it's the best there is to be had absolutely anywhere. Then during my freshman year of high school, there was a minor incendiary device that exploded and destroyed Bep's kitchen. That was my lesson in the meaning of the term "protection money" and what happens when one doesn't pay it.

"Any idea what got this place resurrected?" I asked to deflect the awkwardness of his pulling out my chair for me.

I was refusing to consider this adultery, in spite of the ring on his hand. It was just a doctor interviewing a research subject. I'd even gone so far as to just wash up back at the hotel, letting my hair recurl. I hadn't even bothered reapplying makeup. I was in the comfy jeans and canvas shoes I'd worn on the trip down.

"You've heard of HBC?" he asked.

"The up-and-coming pharmaceutical company?" I nodded. "Yeah, I saw their floral arrangement at the viewing."

"They've brought a lot of jobs to Walkerville over the past ten years," Gene explained. "A lot that was dead seems to be coming back to life, Bep's included."

The waitress arrived. Apparently either Big Hair had never died in Walkerville, or it was making a huge comeback, pun intended. "Whatkinagitchuz?"

Ah, the sounds of home. I briefly considered ordering a shot of whiskey, but Gene's mere presence deterred me. "Just a water, please."

"A what?"

"A..." Oh, right, I was speaking like a foreigner. Time to get my Philly back on. "A *wooder*, please. With lemon."

She glared at me so hard I was afraid her eyeliner might flake off into the food. I think my "please" threw her off. Either that or she thought the lemon was going to be too much luxury for the likes of me.

Gene ordered an iced tea, and then she left us to our menus.

"So," Gene started, "how are your parents? Are they liking Florida?"

I snickered. "Is that the question you wanted to ask?"

He unfolded his napkin. It was burgundy cloth. Bep's had gone hoity toity. Maybe they should've been bombed by the mafia sooner. At least their waitstaff still had the same level of both surliness and Aquanet.

He cringed, his eyes crinkling at the sides. He folded his hands in front of him, on top of the pleather menu cover. "Give me some time. I have to warm up to it."

I caught my eyes fixating on his wedding band and blinked to break my stare. "They're great. Dad retires next year, and Mom found another community college to take her in. They've taken up golfing. How's your family?"

He shrugged and began toying with a piece of vinyl that had broken off the menu binding. "They're okay. My mom has been fighting cancer off and on, but she's in remission again."

I nearly dropped my water. "Oh, Gene, I had no idea. I'm so sorry. What kind of cancer was it?"

"Brain tumors," he said, and he took a drink of his tea. "They've been coming and going for about ten years now.

She's a fighter, though. I keep trying to get her to move, but she still lives in town. That's who I'm staying with. I know she'd love to see you, if you can stop by."

"It would be great to see her, too," I said. I thought of slender, active, blond Gail Marcasian. Then what Gene had just said replayed quickly in my mind. "Wait, you said your mom's still in town. Is your dad okay?"

"He's great. Moved out to Denver when they divorced."

"Divorced!" I shouted in my surprise. A few people at nearby tables shot me dirty looks. Gene looked at me over the top of his glasses.

"I'm sorry," I said much more softly. "Of all the people to split, I never thought it would be your parents. They were so—so—"

An image popped into my mind from younger days, of Gene, his older sister Frances, and their parents kneeling together in Seven Dolors before Mass started. If my family went to Mass, we always got there after the Marcasians and we always left well before they did.

"Catholic?" he finished for me.

"Yeah," I said, "Catholic."

With a sigh, Gene leaned back in his chair and tugged a bit at his shirt collar, even though it was already unbuttoned. "That was my mom's doing. My dad just played along until the role no longer worked for him."

I heard the note of bitterness in his voice as he looked off to the side at nothing in particular.

"That sucks, Gene. I'm really sorry."

He shrugged. "It's been nearly fifteen years now. Most of the burn is gone."

I took another sip of water, letting the lemon's tartness stick on my tongue before I asked another question. "What about Frances? How's your sister doing?"

"She's dead."

I dropped my head in my hands. I thought of gorgeous, golden Frances Marcasian, star of the Mercy Academy basketball team, always surrounded by cute boys from the Salesian Academy where Gene had ended up for high school. I remembered Frances and her long, naturally blond ponytail bouncing as she left Gene and me behind in their living room, us with our Douglas Adams books and our half-eaten bags of cheddar cheese microwave popcorn, the kind that left our fingertips orange.

I lifted my head from my now icy hands. "Dead? Gene, she was only four years older than we were. When did she die? How?"

Somewhere in the distance, I heard the screech of sirens: ambulance, police, fire, or all three for all the cacophony. It was a relatively distant hubbub, so I tuned it out within moments.

So did Gene. He tilted his head, raised his eyebrows, and held his hands out in front of him in a gesture of general surrender. "Long story short, Frances died of blood clots."

The way his voice hung in the air between us, I could tell he had more to say and wasn't being evasive about it. "So that's the short story. Do I want to know the long one?"

Gene sighed deeply and leaned forward over the table. He folded his hands back in front of him and, head lowered, seemed almost like he was praying silently.

"Funny you should ask that," he said. "The long story has to do with why I became a doctor. It has to do with why I chose gynecology as my specialty. It has to do with why my parents divorced and why I'm going around with questions to ask all my female classmates from Seven Dolors Elementary.

I swallowed hard. "Okay?"

Gene nodded as if to acknowledge that I was ready for the rest. "Frances got sick when she was a teenager. She kept getting sick, over and over again, once, sometimes twice a month. It took years for any doctor to figure out what was going on, but the treatment was something my mother was against as part of her faith."

Against as part of her faith? I thought of the birth control pills stashed in my own purse, and I felt something in my own face harden.

Gene went on. "My dad took Frances behind Mom's back. He had Frances lie to my mom for years. He made Frances become a stranger to us. She became a stranger to herself. She fell in with a bad crowd, mostly with—bad guys. A lot of guys. A lot of—bad choices."

I could tell he was having a hard time, going on with this story. I could tell it was hurting him, the way he winced with each word. Finally he stopped and took his glasses off, rubbing the bridge of his nose between his thumb and forefinger. His wedding band glinted in the orange glow of the restaurant's dollar store battery candlelight.

I felt a chill slide over my shoulders and sink into the rest of me. "It's okay. We can change the subject. I didn't mean to upset you."

He lowered his head again and took another bracing breath. Without putting his glasses back on, he looked at me across the table and asked in a suddenly level voice, "Mary Catherine, do you have endometriosis?"

Now I felt chilled and kicked in the gut.

"Is that the question you wanted to ask?" I took a great swig of my water.

"I know you have a fan page on Facebook," he said, "but have you personally friended any of our classmates? Have you seen what's been going on?"

"Careful, Gene," I said, rubbing the back of my neck. "Change the subject that quickly again, and I might get whiplash."

He shook his head. "I'm not changing the subject at all. At the viewing, did you see Heather Fucilla?"

"Well, no, but there were a lot of people I didn't see."

"You won't be seeing her at the funeral tomorrow either. She's in a nursing home."

"What!"

"Blood clots. She stroked out ten days before her wedding. She's been in a nursing home for the past twelve years. Was Turo DiFrancesco there with his kids tonight?"

I shuddered. "I saw that he seems to have reproduced, which is frightening in and of itself."

"I think they're triplets." Gene raised his eyebrows in an "I told you so" look.

"So they're triplets. And?"

"They're triplets," Gene confirmed, "and Lisa Alioto has twins. So does Sophia Marcione."

I let the information sink in, desperately trying to figure out what Gene was trying to tell me. "Is that a lot of multiples for a class of 25?"

"It certainly is," he said. He placed his hands on the table and leaned in with a lowered voice. "I am willing to bet all of those children were the result of infertility treatments of some kind. I further believe that many of the girls who went to our school, and most of the girls in our class, have one of the leading causes of infertility—endometriosis. I want to make sure my suspicions are correct."

I glared across the table at him. "And then?"

He folded his lean arms across his chest. "And then I want to find out why."

"And what," I said, leaning back in my chair to look down my nose at him, "does this have to do with me?"

Gene stared. "What do you mean?"

"I mean," I said, pushing my water glass away from me, "what does this have to do with me? Why are you telling me all these things?"

His chin dropped. He stammered, "Well—you, you were in our class, weren't you?"

"Yes?"

"You're a girl, aren't you?"

"Woman, Gene," I sighed. "I'm a woman."

He slowed his voice down as if talking to a small child. "Given those two conditions, I'd imagine it has everything to do with you. And you still haven't answered my question."

I folded my arms against my chest. "Yeah, funny you should mention the only question you asked me. I mean, I get that you're a doctor and all, but you were also my friend. For a long time, you were—" My voice stalled in my throat, held up by a work crew named Disappointment. "You were my best friend," I managed. "I thought you might take a little more interest in me than my medical history."

In the low light of the restaurant, I saw his face lose some of its already pale color. "Mary Catherine, I—"

I was already ashamed of what I'd said, and I couldn't bear to say any more, much less hear any more. "Forget it," I said, tossing my napkin back onto the table. My red vinyl upholstered chair almost tipped over backwards with the force of my leaving.

"Mary Catherine, please, wait," he said, getting to his feet.

"Great seeing you, Doctor," I said, shouldering my purse. "Good luck finding answers to your questions."

Once I was back in my car, I looked back at the entrance to see if Gene would come after me. He didn't. I couldn't blame him. I put the phone on speaker with one hand and turned the ignition with the other.

Three rings. She had to find her phone. I looked at the time. It was past her third trimester bedtime. As if I couldn't feel worse than I already did.

Staz's voice spoke through the phone, somewhere between sleep and panic. "Cate? What's the matter? Is everything o—"

"Everything's fine," I said. "Nothing's fine. He's a moron. I'm a moron."

I heard Geoff murmuring in the background. "She's fine," Staz replied half out of the phone. "I think it's a drunk dial."

Two state trooper cars sped, lights flashing, down the opposite side of the street.

"I am not drunk dialing. I am disappointed-and-embarrassed-and-ashamed-dialing." I briefly gave her a rundown of the conversation in Bep's, closing with, "I don't know. I feel like I should have given him a chance to get the info he wanted, but I felt so humiliated that I'd—"

"—wanted him to hit on you even if he's married?"

By now I was pulling into my hotel parking lot. I sighed. "Does that make me a bad person?"

"Sweetness, that makes you a human person," she said.

I turned off the ignition and sat back to let Staz give me the mental elixir I so desperately needed. "He was sending you mixed signals from the get-go. Saying he was checking you out but acting all clinical?"

"Well," I admitted, "I am sure I was reading things that weren't there."

"Telling you you're amazing when he shouldn't be saying that kind of thing to anybody but his wife?"

"Staz," I said, passing the two state trooper cars now parked in front of the hotel's main entrance. "He was speaking as a fan."

"And you wanted him to be a man," she said.

"Rhyming and appropriate." I got out of the car and talked as I walked. "I appreciate you not telling me to go back there and apologize."

"What for?" she asked. "You did what you had to do."

"But still," I said, "if I hadn't gotten my hopes up—"

"Which I knew you were doing, even if you acted like you weren't," she said.

"Well," I accused, "with you and Becky egging me on and everything, it was kind of hard not—" I broke off. I had no choice. There were three police officers standing in the mouth of the hallway that led to the elevators. Two were tall-ish state troopers. The one in the middle, however, was local police. He was Bobby Campobello.

"Cate?" Staz asked from the phone that I was now holding down by my waist.

Bobby had tears in his eyes.

Staz said, a little louder, "Cate? You okay?"

"This is her," Bobby said to the troopers. "This is Mary Catherine Whelihan."

Staz's voice shrilled from my phone. "Cate? What's going on?"

With a shaking hand, I brought the phone back to my face. "I don't know. I'll call you back as soon as I'm done talking to the police."

Staz's expletives were cut off as I thumbed the "end call" button.

"Mary Catherine Whelihan?" The officer to Bobby's right said. "I'm Officer Jones. We need to ask you a few questions."

I looked from Jones to Bobby to the other trooper, whose nametag read "Murphy," and then back to Bobby. I wracked my brain for any possible reason that the state police would be looking for me and why Bobby might possibly be crying.

When I'd recovered enough to speak, I said, "Of course, officers. Am I in any kind of trouble?"

The two troopers looked over Bobby's head and exchanged looks that I couldn't read. I felt like my lungs were about to collapse on me. I looked back to Bobby, tried giving him a question with my facial expression.

Bobby sighed. "It's Turo. Turo DiFrancesco."

"What about him?" I asked, annoyance flaring almost through my anxiety.

Officer Murphy stepped forward a little and spoke to me in a gentle, hushed voice. "Arturo DiFrancesco was found dead in the men's bathroom of Our Lady of the Seven Dolors Church tonight."

I almost fell over. Bobby reached up and grabbed my upper arm to steady me.

"It looks like suicide," Bobby said into my ear, so close that his lips brushed my earlobe. His voice halted at every word. "Shot himself. Put a gun in his mouth. He left a note. The note mentioned you."

CHAPTER SIX
IN THE AIR TONIGHT

I had been in the Walkerville police station exactly twice before. Once was when I was in fourth grade. Our class walked down to the station and got a tour. They even locked us in the jail cells, a few at a time. Sister Patrick, whom I probably would have agreed was kind of cool if she hadn't also given me an "F" in gym one quarter, had had a good laugh over certain kids getting locked up. She specifically had Turo DiFrancesco, Gina Maldorone, and Rocco Cargione jailed together. I remember hearing her mutter something about this being the closest thing they'd ever get to a career day, which didn't make much sense to me until a few years later.

The second time was when Tony Vitale had drowned in Quaker Creek. Cutting across the creek from Gene's apartment to my house, I had found the body.

But that was then, and this was now.

They hadn't even asked me any questions other than, "Could you come with us, Miss Whelihan?" I had hoped that I would be taken in Bobby's squad car. Then at least I might have gotten some answers from him. However, I had been placed in the car with Officer Jones. He'd had me ride in the front seat as his passenger rather than his arrest. I took that as another good sign.

Good signs abounded, but still no explanations. I had been left alone and unfettered in the main part of the office. I sat in a wooden chair that creaked every time I breathed. After the first touch, I kept off of the arms of the chair. They felt slick, as if they had been spritzed with cooking spray.

The only other sounds in the office were provided by

the dispatcher, a fifty-something whose teased hair was the failed lavender color of a plastic Easter egg. She sat behind a sliding pane of glass in a little side office near the front door. Next to her pane of glass was another "Go for Gloria!" flyer. The dispatcher did not say a word to me or even look my way. To her I was probably just another drunk or petty thief cooling down.

Beside me was an aluminum desk that was piled with so much detritus that its computer was a mere faceless hulk underneath. There was no visible nameplate, leaving the culprit of the disaster unnamed. Fluorescent lights hummed overhead. It smelled dank like a basement, probably because it was one: Borough Hall was near the base of one of Walkerville's steeper hills, and the police station had been put on the bottom floor, the parking lot sloping down into the nadir of the valley.

I hadn't had a real asthma attack in so many years that I no longer even bothered to keep an inhaler in my purse, but spending this much time in a musty, dusty police station was starting to make my lungs less than happy. After the eleventh or twelfth time I coughed, the door at the opposite end of the office, the door leading back to the jail cells and evidence room I'd seen in fourth grade, opened.

Bobby Campobello poked his head out. His voice sounded tired, apologetic. "You okay out here?"

"Yeah, sorry," I said. I rubbed my throat. "I'm just getting a little wheezy for the first time in ages."

He took a few steps out but didn't release his hold on the door. "My daughter has asthma. Do you need me to call the EMTs, bring you a dragon?"

I gave him a puzzled look. "What's a dragon?"

His café au lait skin went shot with pink. He shook his head, tapped his temple, then gave me an embarrassed smile. "Not a dragon. I meant a nebulizer. For breathing treatments?"

I laughed, which made me cough again. "Probably not, as I don't even know what a nebulizer is. I'll be fine, thanks."

He nodded and ducked back through the door.

I couldn't take it any more. As the door almost slid shut, I called out, "Bobby?"

He looked back at me.

I held my hands up in a gesture somewhere between confusion and surrender. "Is anybody going to tell me why I'm here?"

He grimaced for a second. Then he held a finger up to me and disappeared behind the door once more. A few minutes later he reappeared with a large plastic zip-top bag in his latex-gloved hand. By the time he reached me, I saw that there was a white piece of paper inside. The bag had a white label screened on the side, with red letters spelling "EVIDENCE."

Bobby handed the bag to me. It had the same oily sheen to it as the arms of my chair, but I held on anyway. I then saw that the paper inside was sprayed with a fine mist of miniscule red dots. My throat made an involuntary retching sound.

Before I knew it, the bag slipped from my hands, and Bobby bent to wrap his arms around my shoulders. He patted my back, and I felt his body shudder with a sob.

"He was your cousin," I asked, my mouth muffled on his light blue shirt, "wasn't he?"

He smelled of a cocktail of police station mildew and some light, cinnamon-scented cologne I remembered boys in my high school wearing.

"Yeah," Bobby said. Sighing, he let me go. "I just came from telling my aunt when we picked you up."

He sat down on the edge of his desk, and a small avalanche of papers sifted down to the silver-green linoleum floor. I got up from my chair to help him collect them. Our hands brushed in the mess, and I felt him look up at me for a second, but I didn't look back. What was going on? Bobby Campobello, married, whispering against my ear, hugging me and brushing my hand with his? Wordlessly, I handed the papers back to him but still couldn't shake this strange vibe. I excused it all in the name of grief and shock—both mine and his—as he piled the papers back on his desk.

"Should I try this again?" I forced a nervous laugh and held out my hand for the evidence bag.

Lips white, Bobby nodded. He handed me the bag, and I looked at the suicide note, spattered with the blood of the worst of our class bullies.

The printing was standard word processing product. There was a place on the corner where the ink fanned out as if it had been moistened. Tears? No. The circle of distortion was too wide. It was simply the water that lands on your typical public bathroom sink counter. The note was placed on the water-splashed bathroom counter, and then...

Even when he had been his worst, I hadn't wanted Turo dead. I still didn't. I tried three times to swallow the knot in my throat before I could focus enough on the words of the note to read them. The least sensical part of all was the part with my name.

I have lived with this too long. I already told Tony that it should have been me. I guess I should have told Sister. I'm leaving this note so that I can tell Mary Catherine Whelihan that it shouldn't be her. I can't have her blood on my hands too.

I read the note at least five times before I held the bag

back out to Bobby. "What does he mean, my blood on his hands?" *Did he mean*, I corrected myself, but it was too late.

Bobby frowned. "We were hoping you could tell us."

"Tony," I whispered, reading off the note. I just shook my head. "Do you think he means—?"

I still had trouble saying the name. Bobby finished for me when I halted. "That Tony, Tony Vitale? I assume so. I mean, he mentioned Tony, and then he mentioned you. You are the one who—"

Words seemed to be failing Bobby at this point, too.

"Yeah," I replied, trying to stem the flood of memories of that Saturday evening, finding Tony face down, unnaturally bloated, floating in the creek under the shadow of the railroad bridge.

"I only noticed him because he was wearing his CYO basketball shirt," I heard myself whisper. "I thought one of you left his jersey in the creek."

Bobby rested his hand on my shoulder. It had a weight to it, but it wasn't heavy. It had a warmth but was not feverish. I looked up at him. His dark brown eyes were boring straight into mine. Was he trying to see if I was lying? Was he trying to get me to confess something? Anything? Or did he, like me, just not know what to think?

At that moment, State Troopers Jones and Murphy emerged from behind the metal door. Bobby looked away, standing up with an almost guilty speed.

Murphy spoke directly to Bobby, ignoring me entirely, "You guys okay with this from here on out?"

Bobby shook hands with Murphy. "Yeah, thanks for sticking around."

Jones made this noise that I first thought was a really quick smoker's cough, but then I realized it was his laugh. "Last time I sign on to do traffic duty for a nun's viewing."

"Sorry you got more than you expected, bro," Bobby said, shaking Jones's hand. "I appreciate it. There's nothing more for now. We'll see you tomorrow."

Then the state troopers were gone, leaving me alone with Officer Bobby Campobello.

"Sorry we made you wait," he said at last. "You're sure you can't think of any reason Turo would have named you in his suicide note?"

I shuddered. "Except for the Seven Dolors vestibule tonight, I haven't seen him since we planted Tony Vitale's memorial garden, right after eighth grade graduation. I've barely even thought of him, except when having a social anxiety panic attack."

Bobby flinched at this admission. "Mary Catherine, I want to apologize."

I laughed nervously. "For what? You never did anything."

He nodded. "Exactly. I never did anything to stop people from hurting you. I could have, but I didn't. Can you forgive me for being a coward?"

I looked up into his earnest eyes. These were the kinds of words I had longed to hear from even just one of my classmates: acknowledgement of and remorse for the pain they had caused me. Now that I was hearing exactly these words, I did not know what to say. As much as I wanted to say "thank you," I just couldn't. All I could do was grimace back the tears—tears were something my classmates had tried to mock out of me—and nod.

As I nodded though, a tear rolled out of each eye. I mumbled an apology and turned to get a tissue out of my purse, but Bobby caught my face with his left hand.

He thumbed the tears away from my cheeks. "I'm sorry for everything."

I did not know what to do, what to say. Was this just

him being a very sympathetic friend? Was this just a grief reaction? Or was this something else? Before I knew it, words I didn't know were coming tumbled out of my mouth. "None of this makes sense."

Bobby started as if cold water had been poured down his back. He dropped his hand, chewed his lower lip. With his gloved right hand, he picked up the dropped note and placed it in a large paper envelope back on his desk. "I happen to agree with you. Turo's been hauled in here a few times over the years—"

"That must've made for great conversation at family gatherings," I said.

Bobby laughed briefly. "But it was always little stuff. Bar fights, mostly. He was always angry at everybody else, never at himself."

I nodded. "Sounds like the Turo I knew. Even when Sr. Thomas Marie caught him peeing on my book report in the morning recess yard, it still wasn't his fault."

Bobby froze, looking at me with a very deep frown. "Mary Catherine, where were you around seven PM tonight?"

"I was at Bep's Pizza. Why?"

"And you have witnesses to corroborate your story?"

"My story?" I repeated, incredulous. "I was there having a rather awkward exchange of words with Gene Marcasian. You can't possibly think that I—"

Bobby shook his head and looked away from me. "No, that makes even less sense than Turo doing this at all. But just for your own safety, in case there are questions later, would Gene agree that you were with him at Bep's at the time of the shooting?"

"He should," I said. "I don't think we got so mad at each other that he'd want me framed for murder."

Bobby looked back at me, confused.

"What did you two fight about?"

I sighed and rubbed my tired eyes. My contacts were drying out. "He seems to be on this quest to find out about all the female health problems of every single girl who went to Seven Dolors. I was just another interviewee."

Bobby started. "Female health problems? Like—what? I mean, if I'm not getting too personal."

One look back at Bobby's face, I could tell that this was already personal for him. I looked down at his wedding band before I told him, "He asked if I have endometriosis."

Bobby's eyes widened. "Do you?"

"Yes," I answered without even thinking. I don't know why I felt more inclined to tell Bobby than Gene. Maybe because Bobby didn't seem like he was about to imply that my taking The Pill was a domino leading to a series of "bad choices."

Bobby stared at me, blinking, for what seemed like an entire minute before he said, "I have problems, too."

I let my voice drip with sarcasm. "I assume you don't have endometriosis?"

Bobby hesitated then reached for his desk. He shuffled some papers away and pulled out a small picture in a gold frame. He said, "Let me show you my daughter."

"The one with asthma?"

"The only one," he said. "Never thought me and Stephanie would have a blond kid."

I took the picture from him and studied it. It was a closeup of Bobby, a woman with short, dark brown hair and wide brown eyes, and then a little girl with almond-shaped blue eyes and pale blond hair.

I studied his face for some clue as to what he was getting at. I said, "Well, there are recessive genes that could—"

He pitched his voice to a whisper. "Steph and I tried

for two years before we found out that I had a sperm count of exactly zero.   Keri there is from Kazakhstan.   We adopted her three years ago."

Looking back at the picture, Bobby suddenly smiled like a candle had been lit inside of him, but then his smile faded as he held the picture closer.   "She came to us healthy.   Skinny like a stick, but nothing some good cooking couldn't cure. Since she came home, though, she's got asthma, allergies, and... well, she gets sick a lot."

I didn't know what to say.   His breathing quickened, and I hadn't noticed his eyes getting so bloodshot. Worried he was about to cry again, I just said, "I can tell you love her. You love them both."

I caught myself hoping that reminder would deflect our earlier brushes.   Bobby nodded brusquely and put the picture back on his desk.   "Do you know if Gene is still in town?"

I hesitated a little before I answered.   "He said he's staying at his mom's."

I felt a little bit like a rat fink giving away Gene's whereabouts without his permission, but what reason could I give to keep that information private?   I was just chatting with an old grade school friend.

"Thanks," Bobby said.   "I think I'd better ask him some questions, too."

I guessed from the determination in his eyes that his questions had more to do with his family's health, and less to do with the death of Turo DiFrancesco.

He shook his head as if to clear it, then he reached into a desk drawer.   Pulling out a pad of paper and a pencil, he asked, "Can I ask you a favor, Mary Catherine?"

"Sure."

"Stick around town for a few days.   None of this makes sense, but if Turo's note mentions your name, then having you around to answer some questions might put the pieces together. It should also help get rid of any suspicions that might come your way. *Capiche*?"

I couldn't help but smile. I'd neither heard nor said that word in quite some time. "*Capiche*."

"In the meantime, for your own safety, is there an emergency contact you can give us? Your parents, maybe? A close family friend?"

I told him Staz's name, phone number and address. He jotted it all down on a slip of paper then folded it up and placed it into his shirt pocket. Then he beckoned me to follow him out the door and into the parking lot.

As he drove me back to my hotel, we made small talk. In spite of being in "Group B" in all our reading classes at Dolors, he'd gotten up to speed in public high school. His mom nearly burst with pride when he'd gone to college and majored in criminal justice. Now here he was, second in command of Walkerville's Finest. When it was my turn, I gave him enough of my story to close with, "And now you could say I'm married to my career."

As I stepped out the front passenger door of the squad car, Bobby called after me, "Then I'll see you at the funeral tomorrow?"

It had rained a bit while I was in the station. The door was cold and slick in my hand. "I guess so," I said.

Law enforcement had asked me to stick around. It seemed like I wouldn't be leaving Walkerville just yet after all.

When I finally made it back into my hotel room, the first thing I did was turn my phone back on. Surprise, surprise: Staz had left me exactly 24 texts, five missed calls and three voicemail messages. They started out with a lot of profanity and "call me right now and tell me what's going on or I will drive down there and kick your sorry behind. After I stop to pee five times along the way." About an hour later the texts became a little more worried, "hope you're okay," "oy vey goy vey, now you're really scaring me," and "I'm watching the news to see if you're on it." Finally there were ten identical texts, each reading, "Just call me the second you can. I'm up anyway."

So I did.

"Great googly moogly, Cate!" she shrieked at me the second her thumb hit the "accept" button on her cell. "Are you in jail?"

"No, and I never was," I assured her. I gave her the quickest possible summary of what had happened with Turo.

"I think the suicide was on the news," I heard Geoff say in the background.

"Tell Geoff he should be in bed. He has work in—" I looked at the hotel room's alarm clock. "—four hours."

"If I'm not sleeping, he's not sleeping," Staz snapped. "Besides, it's not like he isn't worried about you, too."

"I'm sorry, guys. I just didn't know if I was even allowed to use my phone while I was in there."

"You didn't even try?" Staz accused.

To get her off my back, I then filled her in on what happened with Bobby.

"Dang, girl," she said. "You've gone from years of zero to two dates in one night?"

"Dates!" I scoffed. "I walked out on the first for not thinking it was a date, and the second was a police officer questioning me in a suicide colored by foul play."

"You know I'm joking. Ow!"

The suddenness of her sound of pain struck me. "You are not allowed into labor until I'm back home. Got it?"

I heard her sigh in the phone. "It's not labor. I pinched something in my back getting back into bed. Geoff, a little help?"

I heard a few more grunts and the gentle rustle of what was probably their comforter. I said, "Well, now I had really better let you two sleep."

"I think I can, now that I know you're not locked up in jail. Or worse, wearing concrete shoes, or making some other mob-related metaphor a ghastly reality."

"I'm not," I said. "At least not yet. But Staz, if you're going to sleep, can I ask you to dream something?"

There was a shocked pause. "Are you writing again?"

Staz was one of my constant research resources, given her knowledge of chemistry—a subject I had nearly failed in high school. Once, when I had been complaining to Staz about having a hard time tightening up a plot hole in the second Alex book, *Alexander McSomething and the Dance of the Dippy Doodahs*, she woke up the next morning having dreamed a way for Alex to use chemistry to solve her problem. So now whenever I needed to bust through a plot wall in an Alex story, I asked Staz to dream something good for me.

"Not exactly," I answered, "but I do have some real life plot holes to fill."

She yawned. Staz is the only person I know who can relax when given a challenge. "Okay. Shoot."

I winced at the word "shoot," unable to help but think of Turo.

"Staz, I need to find out if endometriosis and low sperm count share any potential causes."

"Low sperm count?" she echoed, suddenly sounding quite awake. "What do you need to know that for? There couldn't possibly be something you're not telling me."

"No," I reassured her, "but there is a lot I don't know."

***

To say I barely slept would be obvious. The Mass of Christian Burial was scheduled for ten in the morning, so my finally falling asleep around four hours before that made for a bad situation. I woke feeling less like I'd slept and more like I'd been beaten with an aluminum bat. To make matters worse, I snoozed through my alarm. My eyes flew open at 9:47, which gave me thirteen minutes to shower, dress, do makeup, drive to church, find parking, and then lurk in the back of the church with the rest of the latecomers. I had to stand in high heels that I rarely wore in the first place. I felt like my knees were about to explode. What was even more dire: there was no time for my straightening iron. I had to go with my hair in what Staz calls my "McFro."

I arrived just before the first reading, which means Mass had been going on for about ten minutes already. I was honestly surprised I hadn't been even later. I was yet more surprised to see that the man walking from the front row up to the sanctuary was Gene Marcasian. Strangely, I had ended up standing next to the same bleach-blonde woman in the black dress who'd smirked at me last night when my text alert disturbed the calm.

Gene took his place at the ambo and adjusted the microphone so it would capture his voice. He pushed his glasses up the bridge of his nose, looked down at the lectionary, then looked out at the church.

"A reading from the Book of Daniel," he said.

"At that time there shall arise Michael, the great prince, guardian of your people. It shall be a time unsurpassed in distress since the nation began until that time. At that time your people shall escape, everyone who is found written in the book. Many of those who sleep in the dust of the earth shall awake; Some to everlasting life, others to reproach and everlasting disgrace. But those with insight shall shine brightly like the splendor of the firmament, and those who lead the many to justice shall be like the stars forever.

"The Word of the Lord."

"Thanks be to God," I responded along with the rest of the congregation.

I mumbled along with the responsorial psalm, then watched as Christopher Vitale, he of the CEO alphabet soup and brother of the late Tony, took the ambo for the second reading. His smartly cut dark gray suit made him look quite the gentleman of business, a far cry from the white sport coat and black shirt I remembered him wearing to his own eighth grade graduation. I had been in the back of the church then, too, handing out programs for the service hours I needed in order to receive the sixth-grade sacrament of Confirmation. Standing in practically the same spot now as I had in June of 1984, I couldn't focus on the reading Chris gave. I was too busy watching the back of Gene's head.

My next problem was whether or not to go to communion. While I was no longer a practicing Catholic, I had been a pretty good theology student in my time, so I knew that I was not in the required "state of grace." However, I reasoned, shouldn't God be happy just to have me back in His house? Wouldn't He want me to receive communion? I mean, who were Sr. Thomas Marie and her faculty to tell me what God needs from me? By the time I exchanged the Sign of Peace with the cold hand of Bleach Blonde Glasses Lady, I had made up my mind to go with the flow and take communion.

As I got closer to the front of the church, however, the organ music droning in my ears, I started to break into a flop sweat. I passed the silvered lacquer of my former principal's closed casket, and I could only imagine her stepping out to ask, "Miss Whelihan, when was the last time you darkened the door of the confessional?" Dismissing that thought as the mental raving of a stressed-out psyche, I resolved to keep going and get what I'd come for.

However, as my bleached friend (in my mind I'd started to call her Debbie Harry) bowed before the raised host, I caught a glimpse of Gene out of the corner of my eye. He was sitting in the front row with the other lectors from the Mass, including a well-manicured Chris Vitale.

Gene was kneeling down and looking up into the sanctuary. A set of rosary beads hung from his folded hands. He was frowning. He looked troubled. And whatever it was in his face, or whatever it was that was still bothering me about the way he'd talked to me last night, basically implying that I was a doomed slut like his sister for choosing to treat my endometriosis with birth control... suddenly I wanted nothing to do with him or anything else that he, like his mother, was against as part of his faith.

Then I was standing before the tiny, Indian priest and hearing the words, "The Body of Christ."

My hands had been folded. I dropped them to my sides. I lowered my head. "Just a blessing, Father."

He gently placed the host back into the ciborium in his other hand. He did not even change his expression. He just lightly touched my devil-red curls and whispered a blessing on me.

On my return trip to the back of the church, I saw more familiar faces from my class. Maria DellAmoroso and her son sat with Tina Donato and Pasquale Marchione. Gloria Benevento was here, though she hadn't been at the viewing. She looked very frail and pale, leaning wanly against the back of her pew. I saw a few more classmates, recognized a few other kids from other grades during my time at Dolors.

Then I saw Bobby standing by a doorway. The dark circles under his eyes were telling. Sitting in the last pew nearest him were the woman and child I remembered from his desk picture last night. His wife, Stephanie, while clearly adorable with her sparkling black eyes and pixie-short hair, also looked kind of haggard.

When Mass ended, we were invited to process out to the nearby graveyard. I walked as quickly as I could, trying to keep my distance from as many classmates as possible—especially Gene and Bobby. I kept as far to the edge of the crowd as I could, passing very close to the Tony Vitale Memorial Garden. The *Pieta* replica in the center had been a donation from the Vitale family. The rest of the garden had been shaped and planted by our class and our families during the summer after our eighth grade year. My parents had made me participate, even though I just wanted to forget it all. I'd graduated—wasn't I done with these people? The day of the dedication, when the now late Fr. Sullivan had come out to bless the place, had been the last time I had seen my classmates—all of them except Gene, whom I stopped calling shortly after that. We were in high school. I wanted to be more than friends, and it seemed that "friends" was all he wanted. I moved on.

I turned from the playground and back towards the graveyard. As I returned to the growing crowd, nearly everyone around me was murmuring about what had happened with Turo, what a nightmare it was, and how it was just another proof of The Curse of '87.

The first time I heard someone near me say that, I snapped around to look at that person's face. It was someone quite a bit younger than me, so if she'd gone to Dolors, she would have been at least four years behind me. It had been a small school, so I had pretty much known the names and faces of everyone in a three year radius of my graduating class. Anyway, that person wasn't the last to whisper those words, "The Curse of '87," on our way to the freshly dug gravesite. What did it mean? Where had it come from? And why did so many people—everybody but me, it appeared—seem to know that my class had been cursed?

Since I was one of the first ones out of the church, I was among those who had the longest to wait for the casket to arrive. I spent that time looking around at the gravestones. Many of them were affixed with medallions, in which rested black and white portraits of the deceased resting below. I remembered many of them, as I'd spent a good deal of time playing here back when I had been friends with Gina Maldorone. Well, not really friends. I had been too naive to realize that playing Hide and Seek in the graveyard, with me always hiding and her always seeking but never finding me, was just another form of humiliating the shy, clumsy outsider. I didn't figure things out until fifth grade, with the pancake syrup-hair trick.

It took a while before the congregation had reassembled in the graveyard. I saw Maria, Tina, Pasquale and the others standing together in a cluster off to the side. Gloria was looking quite winded, leaning on a cane in the one hand and with the other taking the arm of another classmate, Rocco Cargione. Near them stood a good buddy of Turo's, Frank Farzza. Frank, dressed in a polo shirt that strained across his shoulders, looked half-angry, half-bored. I kept my distance, glad of my sunglasses.

Gene appeared shortly before the pallbearers. I recognized his mom walking with him. They stopped at a grave on the way. He put his arm around his mom's shoulders as she shook her head and grimaced back tears. His sister's grave, I guessed. She dabbed at her eyes with a tissue and tugged Gene forward. He was frowning and did not follow her at first. Once his feet started moving, though, he was scanning the crowd. He found me. He just nodded. I nodded back and let him move on.

The priest, the aforementioned small, older Indian man named Father Blaise, was now without his microphone. He had to yell against the hills of the graveyard in order to be heard. I heard a few ignoramuses near me complaining about his accent, and I felt a certain kinship toward him. Father Blaise and I were both outsiders, both misunderstood. When all had been said, all prayers prayed, he invited the large crowd back to the church hall for the luncheon prepared by the Ladies' Guild.

I really did not want to go there. I would much rather have stopped at a drive-thru on my way home and collapsed in bed upon arrival, never to see Walkerville again. I turned away from the crowd and looked towards the distant street where I had parked my car. Back at the fringe of the crowd stood Bobby in his uniform. He was not looking my way and was instead talking with an older couple standing near him, holding the crooked elbow of the short woman whose silver head was covered in a lacy white mantilla.

Bobby had just about ordered me to stay last night. So I had to stay in town, but did I have to stay at Our Lady of the Seven Dolors?

"Were you going to try again for that tomato pie?"

I turned, and there was Gene again. I looked over his shoulder. His mom was several yards away, chatting with what appeared to be a pair of small children accompanied by a grandmother. Gail Marcasian was the local librarian, so she was the closest thing Walkerville had to a benign children's celebrity.

"I don't seem to have much of an appetite, which is unusual for me," I said, waving my hands up and down my sides to indicate all the girth I had acquired over the past two decades.

Gene frowned, clearly not admiring my joke. I thought of Bobby asking when I'd become so funny. Apparently Gene did not seem to share that opinion.

A collective movement over Gene's other shoulder caught my attention. It was all of our aforementioned classmates, making their way toward us.

Gene put his hands in his pockets and hunched his shoulders as if he were feeling a sudden chill. "Look, Mary Catherine, I get that you weren't happy about being asked all those questions last night. I get that I was being insensitive, but—"

"You do know what happened to Turo, right?" I interrupted.

Gene stopped the next sentence that was about to come out of his mouth. He shifted his shoulders down a little lower as if dropping a defensive wall. "Yes," he said.

I replied, "I'm not in a mood to be investigated further."

The clump of classmates was almost to us now.

Gene grimaced a bit and nodded, then he asked, "What about being an active part of the investigation rather than a passive one?"

I drew back a bit in confusion. "What do you mean?"

Gene tipped his head backward briefly, indicating the classmates he seemed to know were approaching.

"Come and see," he said.

***

About forty five minutes later, after dashing back to my hotel to finish prettying up, I walked into the dark, cool sanctuary of Pub Mo Thóin. I studied my surroundings as I waited at the hostess station for said hostess to arrive and do her job. Another "Go for Gloria!" poster was taped to the wall next to where I stood. That's when I noticed the last line of said poster read, "Sponsored by Pub Mo Thóin: Home of the 'Go for Gloria' Afterparty!"

The air smelled of fried things and mellowed, meaty shepherd's pie. A busy lunch crowd filled the dining room, a diversity of businesspeople, most of whom seemed to be wearing purple-and-white HBC Pharmaceuticals ID lanyards over their striped golf shirts and rayon blouses. Slender, black-clad, green-aproned waitstaff bustled between tables. Ivory walls over black walnut wainscoting were well-patchworked with maps of Ireland, pictures of thatched cottages and prints of sheep-clad hillsides.

"Just one," the hostess barked, breaking me out of my observations. I looked into her face, and my heart simultaneously sank and floated. The voice had roughened, but there was no mistaking those beady brown eyes. It was Gina Maldorone.

The sinking of my heart was because, well, that's what my heart did every time I saw her ever since she was the one who started the class calling me "Where's The Ham," right around the time those "Where's the beef?" commercials hit the scene.

The floating of my heart was for the pettiest of petty reasons. Gina had gotten fat.

Now, as we reviewed during my interaction with Mr. Celli, I had done more than my own fair share of letting myself go over the past decade or so. Gina, however, hadn't let herself go: she had completely lost her grip. I should have been feeling empathy for her at best, feeling sorry for her at worst. But what I was feeling was sheer delight at the fact that I was only thirty pounds overweight and had a publishing contract, while she was at least three times as much bully as she had been twenty years ago. Her white button-down hostess shirt was the size of a circus tent and still straining at the seams.

When I finally pulled myself together enough to look her back in the eyes, which were even now encrusted with mascara and liquid liner, I caught her looking at me with a sneer on her own face. My heart sank again. I could tell she recognized me. And I could tell that, no matter my appearance, no matter how much thinner or more successful I might have been, she would always, always look down on me.

What was worse and yet more baffling was that it still mattered to me.

"Heeeey, Where's the Ham," she said, squeezing a menu to her ample bosom. She lifted her Roman nose at me. Her thick blond highlights fell away from her foundation-plastered face. "You're back."

I nodded. "Gina. How are you?"

She gave me a moue with her icy pink-glossed lips. "Oh, you know. Nobody stings like the Queen Bee."

I heard myself mutter, "Do queen bees even—?"

She leaned in and cupped an ear in my direction, "What? I can't hear ya."

I gave her a tight smile. "Um, never mind."

She looked me up and down again, found something freshly smirk-worthy in this reappraisal, and then rasped at me in a voice roughened with years of cigarettes and God only knew what else, "They're in the back."

Without another word of explanation she waddled off,

and I could only assume I was to follow her. Her hips pushed the limits of her black Spandex pants—yes, in Walkerville, Spandex had never died, especially in the fashion consciousness of folks like Gina Maldorone. As we walked, though, it became clear to me that Gina was still the most popular girl in school. At every table, men looked up from their menus or away from their conversations. Those few who didn't know her gave her admiring glances. Most of them however seemed to know her well. As we made our way, she tossed private jokes and sandpaper laughter along our path as one would throw bread crumbs to a pursuing flock of geese.

She stopped us at the back of the restaurant. She leaned against the lintel that marked the border into a back room. This room was darker and smaller than the main dining room but still large enough to hold a small stage, a couple of amps, and about a dozen four-top tables. Sitting at those tables were most of my grade school classmates.

"GIIIIIII-NA!" They all called out.

Well, all but Gene and Gloria Benevento. Gloria was leaning against the back of her chair with her eyes closed, her thin hands folded on her lap. At Gina's loud greeting, Gloria's eyes fluttered open, focused, and then fluttered closed again. Pity twisted in my gut. This was not the CYO District 3 Softball Pitching Champ of both 1986 and 1987. This Gloria Benevento was a frail, almost old, woman.

"Gina, you get out of working this shift?" asked another voice.

That was Frank Farzza. He had lived next door to the Maldorones growing up. He was the one who had gone into my desk while Gene, Rosa Trinaglia and I were in Sister Thomas Marie's office for our advanced language arts class. Frank had taken advantage of my absence, and the regular teacher's stepping out to take a phone call, and used my ruler to measure a certain part of his anatomy. Maria told me at recess that his bold measuring had inspired all the boys in our class to pass around my ruler and do the likewise for themselves. Apparently Frankie Puziano and Franco Zittiano had tied for first place.

"Partying don't pay for itself." Gina shrugged at Frank.

There were cheers of approval. I felt myself smile awkwardly as I looked for a place to sit. Maria was sitting with Lisa Alioto and a man I didn't recognize, probably Lisa's husband. Bobby was standing back in a corner, in uniform still from the funeral. He glanced at me and then deliberately looked away. He held his hands behind his back, talking with a much older-looking and very much thinner version of Rocco Cargione. Frank Farzza stood next to them, alternately listening and grumbling his side of the conversation, his beefy arms folded across his brick wall of a chest.

I found Gene, who was not sitting by himself as I imagined he might. Instead he and a now empty bottle of some local microbrew were sharing a table with Tina and Pasquale. The couple was holding hands, glasses of water sweating on the table in front of them. Pasquale was gesturing animatedly with his free hand, talking excitedly but in hushed tones to Gene. Tina had tears rolling down her face, but through them she was smiling. Gene reached out with both hands and clapped them each on the upper arm. Then he nodded and said something with a small, confident smile. Pasquale nodded back, then dragged his sleeve across his own moist eyes.

As Tina buried her face in Pasquale's shoulder and Pasquale nuzzled the top of her head, Gene looked up and found me lurking in the doorway.

I looked away, embarrassed that I had been caught

watching what seemed to be such an intimate, perhaps even doctor-patient confidentiality moment. But Gene called my name and I saw him beckon me over.

As I made my way to their table, though, people stopped, stood up and greeted me with hugs. It was that first hug with Maria DellAmoroso all over again: at worst these people had been downright cruel to Gene and me, at best had merely stood back and let us be tortured. Why all the nicey-nice now? Or, if they were going to be nice, why do so without any apology or at least acknowledgement of what we had all been to each other as children—namely, my role and Gene's as their punching bags? Gina may still be the Queen Bee, but at least she wasn't putting on an act.

To my hugging classmates, I was no more than cordial, knowing full well that my distance would be seen as snobbery, not self-preservation. I didn't care so much about their opinions right now. I just wanted to find out what Gene was going on about: that is, my being an active part in the investigation of Turo DiFrancesco's death.

"So," I said to Gene once I finally reached him, "fancy meeting you here."

He smiled and sighed, the kind of sigh you hear somebody give after they've dropped a heavy burden.

"Are you okay?" I asked.

With his left hand he scratched his temple. His wedding ring taunted me. "I'm fine. Just doing some work off the clock. I think I'm going back to the bar. Can I get you—"

"Gene," Bobby interrupted, having left his corner and now standing in the middle of the room. Our classmates and their attendant significant others hushed. "I think everybody's here that said they'd try to make it. Do you want to get started?"

Gene gave me an apologetic look.

"No beer for the weary?" I said. "I can go get one for you. What's your poison?"

Gene shook his head. "No, Mary Catherine. I need you here for all of it."

Gulp. I tried laughing off the gravity of this remark. "Even if it means I'm not getting you beer?"

Gene paused thoughtfully for a second before leaning towards my ear so that only I could hear him. "Can I take a raincheck on that?"

Before I could answer, though, Gene touched my shoulder briefly then walked over to where Bobby was standing in the middle of the room. Gene cleared his throat, scratched his ear nervously once more, and then he began.

His voice was quiet and strong. "Hey, everybody. I'm sorry we got together under such grim circumstances. I know most of you are on Facebook, so you already know that I'm an OB/GYN out of St. Gerard Medical Center in Harrisburg. I specialize in restorative treatments of fertility problems."

Restorative? I thought to myself. What did that mean?

"Because of this," Gene continued, "I've spent the past several years studying the genetic and organic causes of such problems."

"Yo, speak English," Frank Farzza barked in his low, denasal voice.

Half of the room laughed appreciatively, but Pasquale Marchione looked over his wife's shoulder and said, "Shut up, Farzza. Let him talk."

All I could hear in the ensuing silence of the room was the mad hammering of my heart. This was the kind of exchange that led to afterschool fights down in Quaker Creek Park. All eyes were on Frank. Frank glared back, but he re-folded his arms and leaned against the wall once more.

Throughout all this, Gene was standing stock-still, breathing evenly and not showing a single sign of his calm being ruffled. I envied his nerve. I was a quivering mess for his sake, and I wasn't even the one doing any of the talking.

"Frank makes a good point, though: that we should get to the point. We've all heard about 'The Curse of '87.'"

Everyone else in the room nodded, even the supposed-spouse of Lisa Alioto. Sheepishly, I half-raised my hand.

"Sorry," I said, "but what is The Curse of '87?"

Gloria Benevento's eyes flew open. She gaped at me. Her voice was softer than a down feather. "You don't know about the curse?"

Frank Farzza thudded the back of his head against the wall behind him. "Aren't you on Facebook?"

"Of course she is," said Jennifer Russo, a few tables away with her husband. "I've 'liked' her fan page. She posts something on there at least once a day."

In the face of such a compliment, I felt myself blush hot in the dark, cool room. Still, I had to admit, "Actually, that's not me. That's my publisher's PR department."

I got a few looks of disbelief at my obvious arrogance, but Gene didn't give me time to respond. Hands outstretched, Gene challenged our classmates, "Well, somebody tell her about The Curse of '87."

There was a moment's pause while heads lowered and bodies shifted uncomfortably. Finally, Gloria Benevento said, "Well, for starters, I've been fighting breast cancer off and on for the past ten years."

I gasped. "Gloria. I'm so sorry."

Rocco, sitting next to Gloria, patted her softly on the shoulder.

Then he said, "And I have non-Hodgkins Lymphoma."

I was mute with shock.

"And," said Lisa Alioto, "anybody here who's had trouble getting pregnant—"

"Or staying that way," interjected Tina Donato.

Lisa nodded. "Raise your hand."

All of the girls, now women, in the room raised their hands. It occurred to me that, had I been married to anyone besides my career, my hand might have been up too.

However, Pasquale Marcione held his pregnant wife's other hand, and both he and Tina were smiling at Gene. Before I could guess why, more diagnoses came forth.

"I have Lupus," said Donna Illardo.

"So do I," said Anthony Nuccio.

"My cousin, Tina Fagliano? She couldn't make it," said Jennifer Russo, "but both my twins and her little boy, all of them—"

Her voice caught suddenly. Clearly, she wasn't expecting this forthcoming admission to make her cry like it did. Once she finally pulled herself together enough to speak, she said through trembling tears, "All three of them are autistic."

Nods and soft sounds of sympathy filled the room. I felt my fingers go to my lips, as if that could contain all the shock I was feeling.

Gloria breathed heavily then said as loudly as she could, "And you all remember when Gina was sick. She couldn't make senior prom because of the radiation."

All the kids who'd gone with Gina and Gloria to Walkerville Regional Public High School nodded their heads at the memory. All, that is, except Frank Farzza. He was too busy glaring at Gene.

"Not to mention Tony Vitale," Bobby added, his voice just barely audible, "And now Turo. That's all a whole lot of bad for a class of 25 kids."

I looked around and ran through the roll of our graduating class. I asked, "Has anybody heard from Rosa Trinaglia?"

Uncomfortable glances were exchanged, and the room deepened into silence. Bobby Campobello stood up straight in his uniform and announced, "Rosa's family moved away during high school."

By the tiny smirks flitting through the room, I could tell there was more to the story.

"What about you, Marcasian?" Frank Farzza said a little too loudly. He left his place against the wall and began to advance on Gene. "You getting us all here to spill our guts for you. You such a brainiac that the curse spared you?"

Color rose in Gene's face. He crammed his hands into his pockets. "I don't think you could say that, Frank. Not when my mom has had brain tumors and my sister is dead."

A few heads around us nodded empathetically. Last night's anger was now gone. All I wanted to do, wedding ring or not, was hug all the pain out of my old friend Gene.

Still advancing, Frank said, "So everybody who went to Dolors has problems. What's your point?"

I saw Gene's whole body tense up like a guitar string being tuned too tightly, ready to snap at the slightest brushing. He first addressed Frank, but he still continued to look from one face to another as he spoke.

"My point is that the more I know what has become of us all as adults, the more it looks like something went very seriously wrong in Walkerville in the 1980s. Our class, for whatever reason, seems to be bearing the brunt of it. I don't know what the cause of it all is, or if there even is one single cause. But I think we owe it to not only ourselves, but our future generations—"

Gene nodded meaningfully at Jennifer Russo.

"—to find out what it is, to get ourselves and our..." Strangely, Gene paused here and winced for a moment. "...our children the help and healing, and protection if possible, that we all deserve."

That was the first moment, Gene stumbling on the word "children," when I realized that Gene's wedding ring might indicate children as well as a wife.

Frank Farzza planted himself too close to Gene and said, "You know what? I think you're full of it. You're not trying to help anybody but yourself."

Pasquale rose from his seat and growled warningly, "Frank, man. Don't."

Frank leaned in closer. Gene did not flinch. I could see him breathing faster, his jaw grinding as he looked straight down into his antagonist's eyes.

Frank jerked his chin up at Gene and shouted to all the room, "Youse know why he's doing this, right? There's no Curse of '87. He's just trying to make up for hiding away at college while his slut of a sister—"

Gene moved so quickly that I didn't even see his fist make contact with Farzza's jaw. The only reason I know that Gene made the first move was because Gene had stepped back, shaking the impact out of his right hand, while Frank Farzza lay sprawled out on the floor of the back room of Pub Mo Thóin.

"GENE!" I screamed.

Frank scrambled back to his feet, knocking over two chairs as he did so. Gene held his ground, leaning in with his fists ready for another go. In seconds, I found myself at Gene's side, throwing my palm across his chest, pushing him away from Frank.

Bobby was moving as quickly as I was to stop Frank. "Bro, think about it," I heard him say. "Your parole officer is not gonna like this."

I felt Gene breathing hard, his chest heaving beneath my open hand. I could even feel the square of his brown scapular underneath the fabric of his shirt. Afraid to release Gene, I looked over my shoulder at Bobby and Frank. Frank turned to the side and spat out a mouthful of blood, which hit the tile floor with a snap.

Bobby caught my eye. "Get him out of here," he said.

I looked up to Gene, his nostrils flaring, his eyes wide and intent on Frank.

"Come on, Gene," I said, taking his arm and tugging it fruitlessly. "Finish this another time."

"Damn right we'll finish it," Frank said.

"Frank, back off," Bobby said through gritted teeth.

I felt Gene's body drop the slightest bit of tension. It was just enough for him to follow the pull of my hands, out of the back room, through the main dining room, past Gina Maldorone at the hostess station.

"Where you two going?" Gina called after us. "Youse playing Spin the Bottle in there?"

We left her uproarious laughter behind us as we stepped into the hazy light of the lunch hour. I did not let go of Gene's arm as I surveyed our surroundings. He needed to cool down, quite literally: I could see the knuckles on his right hand swelling. Across the street and a few doors down was a coffee shop. I dragged Gene inside and asked the barista for a bag of ice and two iced coffees.

"Make mine with almond milk, please," Gene said.

The barista smiled a patronizing smile. "Will soy milk be all right?"

Gene's lips went tight. "Coconut milk? Rice milk?"

The barista shook her head mournfully. "Sorry, we only have soy."

Gene nodded. "Just the coffee, then."

I was a little startled by all this. "What was that about?"

"I'll explain later," he said.

The barista asked, "You want the ice separate or in the coffees?"

"You're kidding me, right?" I asked.

A few minutes later I took our drinks, a plastic shopping bag of ice, and a seething Gene to a small table in the back.

Shaking his head, Gene took the ice bag and placed it on his knuckles. "I swore I wasn't going to let them get to me. I swore I was going to be the bigger man."

"Like that's hard." I snorted. "The biggest one of them is five-four. You can't help but be the bigger man."

Gene eyed me in disbelief. "Remind me why we didn't vote you class clown for the yearbook."

"Because Rocco Cargione's armpit farts were just that realistic," I replied. "Oh, and I was too afraid of mockery to say anything to anyone but you."

Gene laughed. "True."

"Here," I said, "let me see your hand."

With his ringed left hand, he lifted up the ice bag. His knuckles were purpling already.

"Dang, Gene," I said. "That'll teach them to make fun of you for taking karate lessons."

Gene had his back facing the door, so he did not see the next customer enter the coffee shop. Giant glasses, bleach-blonde hair, black dress, thin as a stick: it was the same woman I'd already bumped into two times now since my return to Walkerville. Something about the way she moved, stiffly but with a command of the room, was familiar, but I couldn't place it any more than I could place her face. Maybe it was just something so "New York City" about the way she dressed and moved. She was the kind of person I encountered by the hundreds whenever I went up there.

When she caught me staring at her, I looked away.

"Are you okay?" Gene asked, frowning at me.

"Yeah," I said, "just saw a stranger from the funeral is all."

His frown deepened. "That's vague."

His criticism startled me. "Vague?" I accused. "Vague is better than conflicting."

He drew back. "Who's being conflicting?"

I coughed out a laugh. "You are! Checking me out and admitting it? Asking me out to dinner and calling it 'research?' Telling me you needed me over at that pub? Telling me all about your mom and your dad and your sister and all their tragedies, but meanwhile, here you are with that nice, shiny ring on your finger and not a word about the woman who gave it to you."

Gene's eyes widened and he leaned back further in his chair, putting distance between us. "Mary Catherine, you could have just asked me if I'm married."

When he put it that baldly, my embarrassed fury immediately turned to just plain old, unadorned embarrassment. I pulled myself together enough to ask,

"Well, are you?"

He sighed and with his left hand rubbed his eyes under his glasses. When he still didn't answer right away, I blurted, "Let me guess: it's complicated?"

He lowered his hand and shook his head. "No, actually, not complicated at all."

"So you are married."

"I don't know."

I gaped at him. When he didn't reply, I found myself shaking my head. "You don't know if you're married?"

He looked off into the space behind us and lifted his coffee. Before taking another sip, he said, "That's right."

"Gene, can I give you a piece of advice?" I asked.

Gene raised his eyebrows.

"It would've been simpler if you'd just said, 'It's complicated.'"

He put his coffee down. "I'm waiting on an annulment."

"So you're divorced."

"Well, yes, in the eyes of the State of Pennsylvania."

"So if you're not carrying a torch for her still, why wear the ring?"

His eyes narrowed. "How do you know I'm not carrying a torch for her?"

I leaned in toward him, dropping my voice to a mock-conspiratorial whisper. "Because your body language is angry and annoyed, not despondent. If a writer can do anything useful in real life, it's to analyze body language to get to the emotion behind it."

He lifted one skeptical eyebrow. "What if I'm lying?"

I shook my head and admitted, "Okay, I'm not a human lie detector, but I'm not bad when I catch people with their guard down."

"So," Gene asked, "do I have my guard down?"

We looked at each other. His eyes held a challenge, but there was no animosity within them. His expression was even but not blank. It was the kind of moment where I might have just leaned over and kissed him, for the electricity between us.

If only he knew whether or not he was married.

I was the first to break the gaze. I distracted myself with another sip of iced coffee. "I think we've always had our guard down. That's probably what made us such easy targets for our classmates."

"You have it all wrong," a voice said from behind Gene's chair.

Gene leaned to the side and craned his neck around. I likewise angled myself so I could see around him.

"Look, Gene," I said. "It's Debbie Harry."

The woman laughed lightly and tossed her nearly white hair over her black-clad shoulder.

Gene eyed her but spoke to me. "This isn't Debbie Harry."

I was about to snap, "Well, duh!" But now that she was close enough that I could look her in the face and see what was hiding behind her glasses, my brain was shuffling through its own album of mug shots. I knew her from somewhere. I had seen her headshot in black and white multiple times but had never been introduced.

"You're right," I said. "This isn't Debbie Harry. This is Trini Ross."

The woman nodded but her thin lips did not smile.

"Who?" Gene asked.

In my purse, I heard my phone buzz with a text from Staz. I ignored it.

"Gene, this is the writer, Trini Ross, known for her literary fiction set in the Tuscan countryside," I answered. "It's nice to meet you in person, Ms. Ross. We share an agent, Becky Ulrich?"

She nodded again but remained silent.

"Sorry," Gene said, turning to her. "Apparently I only read medical journals and chapter books. It's nice to meet you. I'd offer to shake your hand, but—"

He indicated his ice-bound punching hand.

"Oh, that's all right, Doctor," she said in a soft voice. "We've already met."

I studied her face and waited for some indication of where they'd met before, but I couldn't imagine what she would say. I mean, she and I ran in some similar circles, even shared an agent, and I had never met her.

Or, I suddenly realized, maybe I had. I stopped remembering headshots I'd seen inside book flaps and on Becky's office wall. Instead images of the white, brown and navy blue plaid Dolors uniforms flitted into my mind, along with images of the faces that floated above our Peter Pan collars.

It seemed Gene was conjuring up similar memories.

"You're not Trini Ross," he said. "You're Rosa Trinaglia."

At this revelation, Trini, or Rosa, looked over her shoulder to see if anyone were watching. The coffee shop was empty of anyone except the three of us and the trio of baristas.

She turned back to us. "I just told you, you got it all wrong. Don't you want to know what 'it' is?"

She held a tiny white cup of espresso. I could smell its strength as she lifted it to her lips, her burgundy nails glistening on the miniature handle.

I didn't answer her question, though, and I continued to ignore the texting buzz of my phone in my bag. I was just arriving at an answer to a question of my own.

"The poppy!" I pointed at her accusingly. "There was a red poppy in Sister Thomas Marie's casket at the viewing. You put it there, didn't you?"

She gave me a reproving glare. "Ah, Mary Catherine. You haven't changed a bit."

I straightened up. "And what does that mean?"

She shrugged. "It means you're still so caught up in your own mind that you don't bother to wonder at the minds of others."

Gene looked back at me and caught what had to be my offended expression. He cleared his throat, then shifted over to the chair next to mine. With his left hand, he gestured to his now empty chair. "Care to join us, or will that blow your cover?"

She gathered up her cup, saucer and spoon. Even though her designer heels popped like gunfire against the shop's brown ceramic tiles, she still moved like a breath of air. She had always been tall and slender with certain superiority about her. Now, as she settled across from me, I could see through her large glasses that she had cultivated a distinguished calm over her features. She wore no makeup but a whisper of lip shimmer. She still looked smooth and fresh. I was even more jealous of her now than I had been in junior high. To my mind, she'd had it all then. Now she had it all and then some.

She settled into the seat across from me. I appreciated Gene making himself a wall between us.

"Okay then, Rosa, or Trini, or whoever you are," I began. "What is this 'it' that we're not getting?"

"Whoever I am?" she demanded, eyebrows arched. "That's amusing, coming from someone else who uses a pen name. It seems like only our Dr. Marcasian here hasn't been hiding anything."

"I wouldn't go that far," I muttered.

Gene gave me a sidelong glare.

"The 'it' to which I'm referring? It's your guard," she said. "Both of you."

"Our guard?" I echoed stupidly.

Eyebrows raised meaningfully, she took a soft slurp of espresso. "What were you talking about when I interrupted your little tryst?"

I smacked my open hand on the table so hard that Gene jumped in his seat a little. "Okay, first? Not a tryst. It's just two old friends having coffee."

"And ice," Gene added.

"Second, for someone who came back to town in a disguise, you're not really in much position to talk about the quality of anybody's defenses."

Gene cleared his throat again. "Um, Mary Catherine?"

I waved a "shut up" hand in his direction and continued my tirade at Rosa-Trini. "I mean, really, what is that, a wig? And those glasses?"

"Mary Catherine?" Gene said a little more forcefully this time.

"Those glasses look like something out of *Napoleon Dynamite* only without the charm. What's so horrible here in Walkerville that you have to hide under all this?"

Rosa put her cup back in its saucer, then placed both on the table in front of us. "Doctor, do you think you can fill her in?"

Okay, that was puzzling. I turned to Gene.

"I think this is the first time she's back since—" He halted.

"Since?" I prompted.

"Since her family entered witness protection?" Gene looked to Rosa for confirmation, which she gave with a slow, deep nod.

Rosa tilted her head. "Or, as the family likes to call it, 'The Program.'"

I thought of Bep's Pizza and their neglected protection money. I turned to Rosa. "Was your family, you know, connected?"

"Again," she said, rolling her eyes, "still so caught up in your own little world that you miss the bigger picture."

I squirmed, and my rickety coffee shop chair squeaked in protest. "And I guess you're the bigger picture?"

She shook her head. "Hardly. But at least I know there is one."

Gene's ice bag rattled as he changed position to face her better. "What do you know?"

Rosa tinked her tiny spoon against the side of her espresso. "Mary Catherine, you saw my poppy, and I saw yours. What made you pick that for your arrangement?"

I replied, "It's what Sister Thomas Marie always told me."

"'Lop off the tall poppy,'" Gene quoted. "It's what she

said whenever somebody made Mary Catherine cry."

"Or beat you up in the recess yard," I countered.

"Or whenever my parents took my books from me," Rosa said.

Gene and I both turned on her, astonished.

Behind the huge glasses, I could see Rosa's eyes glistening. "I loved Sister Thomas Marie," she said. "I wasn't just another mafia princess to her. She refused to let me see myself that way, either. She was the first person in my life who saw me as something more than just an extension of the family. So when they told me they didn't want anybody to think I was weird, Sister said they were just—"

"Lopping off the tall poppy," Gene finished for her.

Rosa nodded.

We sat there in silence. I had never thought of Rosa Trinaglia as anything other than a popular snob. She was rich, pretty, and always got invited to every single party that any classmate ever had. She never stood alone against a wall at a CYO dance. And now she was a critically acclaimed author, crying in a Walkerville coffee shop about being told by her family what a weird child she was. My world was pretty much rocked with that.

"I loved Sister Thomas Marie," Rosa repeated. "And I have a bad feeling that she didn't die of natural causes."

I felt Gene suck in his next breath. I'm not sure I was breathing at all. I was thinking of Turo's note. *I guess I should have told Sister.*

"She was pretty old," Gene said, doubt heavy in his voice.

Rosa ignored his tone and nodded as if he were in agreement. "Which would have made it all the easier to cover up."

I'm leaving this note so that I can tell Mary Catherine Whelihan that it shouldn't be her.

"Can't you tell the police?" I asked.

"Not if I want to stay alive."

"Not even Bobby?" I asked hopefully. "He's always been one of the better guys in our class. He's a cop now. Maybe he—?"

Rosa smirked. "I don't think I'll be talking to Bobby Campobello any time soon. I'm not sure you should, either."

"He questioned me last night," I blurted, "about Turo."

Rosa scowled. "What did you tell him?"

I held my hands up in a "don't shoot" pose. "I didn't have anything to tell. We just talked about Turo, Bobby's daughter's health, and, well, I hate to sum it up this way, but I guess we talked about The Curse of '87."

I wasn't sure if I should mention Bobby's apology and his overall manner with me, so I kept it to myself. There was no question as to his marital status, after all.

Gene added, "He asked me today about his health."

"By the way, Doctor," Rosa said, rising from her seat, "you might find it interesting to know that I don't seem to have been all that badly affected by our so-called curse."

Gene turned on her with a puzzled expression. He took the ice bag off of his hand. "What does that mean?"

"I mean that my father, who was, as Mary Catherine so delicately put it, 'connected,' did a lot of construction contracts for the company that bought the old Walker Chemical factory."

I watched Rosa give Gene a pointed look, which caused Gene's face to lose its color.

"Hantzell-Brace-Courton Pharmaceuticals," Gene answered.

"Okay, so?" I demanded as Rosa and Gene continued their face-off. "What do we do with that information?"

She ignored me and addressed Gene. "You take that as

the answer you've been bothering all our nice classmates for."

Gene frowned and ran his tongue thoughtfully behind his closed bottom lip.

Rosa stepped back from our table, her sharp heels clicking once, twice against the tiles.

"Wait," I said, getting up from my chair as if to stop her. "Where do you think you're going, just dropping these bombs and then flying off? Don't you want to help us?"

Looking back at us over her shoulder, Rosa said, "My mom was from Tuscany, but I'm still half-Sicilian."

"And?" I asked.

She lifted her shoulders just enough to make herself look even more elegantly formidable. "It looks like a friend of mine has been whacked. I have work to do."

Gene and I stared after her as she clicked out of the coffee shop and slid out the door back into daylight. In the doorway, she replaced her giant fake glasses with even larger sunglasses then disappeared from sight.

It took another minute before Gene and I looked at each other again. I was the first to speak. "So even if we hadn't just been told that we might not be able to trust the local police, I don't even think she gave us enough for them to go on. So, again I ask, what are we to do with that information?"

Gene stood up and took his empty iced coffee in one hand, the sloshing bag of half-melted ice in the other. "Hey, Mary Catherine?"

"Yeah?"

"Would you like to go to the library with me?"

I froze and studied Gene's face. His eyes were intense, his brow furrowed, and his lips formed a thin, straight line. He was formulating a plan.

Knowing I should be running the other way, I stood up

and shouldered my purse. "When have you known me to turn down a trip to the library?"

On my way back to my car, before meeting Gene at our next stop, I finally checked my texts. There were three, all from Staz:

Okay, the first fertility-wrecking chemicals that came to mind were dioxins, formaldehyde, DEHP, chlorpyrifos.

I think I spelled that last one right. They've all been used in insecticides and herbicides, BTW.

How are things? Miss u. Geoff @meeting2nite.

I texted her back. *Herbicide is a fancy word for "weed killer," right? I'm doing... okay.*

My phone buzzed again as I pulled into the library parking lot. Staz: *Y, fancy weed killer word. Call me l8r.*

Ok, I typed back. *Going to library with Gene now.*

Gene was already standing by the glass doors into the Riding County Free Library: Walkerville Branch. The late afternoon sun was casting his face in shadows, making his cheekbones and firm chin look especially well-chiseled.

My phone buzzed again. *Yum. Nerd love. Nerd adultery?*

I'll explain that later, I replied before slipping my phone back into my purse and climbing the steps to meet Gene.

"Ready?" he asked as I reached the top step.

"No," I replied, "but why should that stop me?"

Gene reached for the door handle to hold it open for me, but he stopped short. "Are you sure you're feeling all right? I mean, I know you're under stress, but—"

"Gene, 'stress' doesn't even begin to cover it."

"Still, you've seemed extra-manic as the day has gone by. You were particularly shrill with—"

He stopped and glanced up into the corner of the awning. I followed his gaze and saw a security camera fixed on us.

"—at the coffee shop," he finished.

I sighed and rubbed my temples. I had the start of a headache from lack of sleep and then from having had caffeine in the middle of the afternoon. That and, given where my month's supply of The Pill was, I was heading into PMS-land. "Sorry. This is all just hitting me at the wrong time."

Gene opened his mouth to say something but seemed to think the better of it. Instead he said, "If you think there's anything I can help with, let me know."

"Working off the clock again, Doctor?"

"If you need me to." He stepped back and let me through the door.

I passed inside and through the security detectors flanking the entrance. The first thing I noticed about the place was that it had been completely re-designed.

"It smells wrong," I said under my breath.

Gene looked down into my face. "Wrong how?"

I remembered the dizzying perfume of the stacks, paper in varying states of decay, the warm musk of the copy machine, the overpowering floral essence of urinal cakes seeping out of the bathrooms and into the main body of the library. All of these smells were gone.

I hissed into Gene's shoulder, "It smells like computers that need dusting."

I followed Gene into the reference room, just past the entry into the children's section. We passed the room with its stacks of carpet squares and a whole display devoted to Roald Dahl. As children's librarian, this room was Gene's mom's empire.

No sooner had I thought that, when a pair of slender,

tanned, ringless hands slipped up from over Gene's shoulders and covered his eyes.

Gene's mouth formed a wry smile. "Hi, Mom."

Mrs. Marcasian leaned over his shoulder, smiling mischievously. The sight of her face clashed so directly with my memories of her that at first I was struck speechless. Mrs. Marcasian was more than merely aged. She was just so very changed. Gene's wry smile was a mirror of hers, but where Gene's face was lean, Mrs. Marcasian's seemed just this side of gaunt. There was also a droop to the right side of her face, a droop so slight that had I not known her so well so long ago, I might not even have noticed. That must have been from her tumors, I thought.

I was still gaping in stunned silence when Mrs. Marcasian's eyes lit upon my face, and she traded her teasing smile for a joyful one. As she shouted, "Mary Catherine!" and pulled me into her arms, it occurred to me that, no matter what illness, time, or other hardships might do to her outer appearance, she still had a delight at living that I could not remember seeing in anyone else I had ever met. It was better than a hug from my own mother.

"It's so good to see you, Mrs. Marcasian," I said when she finally let me go. The fluorescent lights above reflected softly off of the silver edges of the Miraculous Medal she wore on a chain around her neck.

"And it's good to see you, my dear. I'd offer you some of that cheddar microwave popcorn that used to turn your fingernails orange, but I don't think we have any in the break room."

Even Gene snickered at this.

Mrs. Marcasian beckoned us to follow her to her desk in the new children's library room, but Gene stopped her.

"Actually, Mom, Mary Catherine and I are here to do some research."

Mrs. Marcasian stopped short at this. Her smile fell, her face darkened. "What kind of research?"

Gene lifted his eyebrows.

Mrs. Marcasian scowled at her son, then biting her lip, looked at me. "I realize you two are fully grown adults, but be careful, Mary Catherine."

"Me?" I tried to laugh. "What about Gene?"

She turned her blue eyes—just like Frances' blue eyes, now forever closed—on her son and his stubborn frown. "I've already told him to be careful. Now I want him to take care of you."

Gene leaned down and kissed his mother on the cheek. "Pray for us, Mom."

She pursed her lips, but she lifted her fingers to her Miraculous Medal, and that joy returned to her eyes. "Always."

An eight year-old boy in a striped shirt stepped next to Gene's mom. Then he tapped on her elbow. "Missuz Mar-kay-zann?"

"One moment, Michael, and I'll meet you over by the green computer." She turned back to me and Gene. "I'll let you two get to your research. Oh, and Mary Catherine, please do stop by tomorrow night, if you can? It would be great to catch up."

For the first time on this return trip to Walkerville, I received an invitation to catch up that I trusted was sincere. "I would love to, Mrs. Marcasian. Thanks."

Mrs. Marcasian turned back to her area, and Gene beckoned me to follow him into another room, an addition to the library since last I'd been here. So much had happened in twenty years. It then hit me how much had happened in the past twenty-four hours: the viewing, my

fight with Gene, Turo's suicide, Sister's funeral and burial,
the impromptu Class of '87 reunion at the pub, the
discovery of Rosa and all she told us. I was suddenly very
tired. I rubbed my temples again and closed my eyes.
When I opened them again, we had reached a room with a
Maginot line of computers. A glimmer of brass caught my
eye. Perched and shining atop the room's sign-in podium
was a plaque.

The Friends of
Riding County Public Library: Walkerville Branch
Gratefully Acknowledge the Generous Gift from
Hantzell-Brace-Courton Pharmaceutical Corporation
That Made This Technology Annex Possible.
Dedicated August 1998

I touched the plaque with my forefinger and caught
Gene's eye once he'd finished writing his name and his
library card number on the appointed line. He raised his
eyebrows then passed the sign-in clipboard to me.

"I bet you still have your library card."

I felt my face go scarlet. "What makes you think that?"

He pulled the clipboard out of my reach. "If you don't
have a card, you'll have to apply for one in order to use a
computer. That'll take about twenty minutes. I might
have found everything I need by then."

I ducked my head and fished my old paper card out of a
back compartment of my overstuffed wallet. Gene cleared
his throat as if holding back laughter.

Nerd love indeed, I thought.

At this hour on a weekday, the lab was bustling with
giggling preteens who were not doing their homework as
I'm sure they had told their parents. There were two
computers available, but they were separated by small

oceans of kids in sideways baseball hats and skirts that barely deserved the name. I wondered why The Technology Generation was gathered in the public library, not at home on their own laptops and tablets.

"Gene, I have a laptop back at my hotel room. Couldn't we just—"

"We could," he interrupted in his library voice, "but you'd be using the hotel wireless, right?"

I thought of Rosa-Trini in her disguise with her furtive over-the-shoulder glances. "Which would be more easily caught than over these landlines?"

"I hope so, anyway," he said.

"Doesn't signing in at the Technology Annex check-in desk blow the whole cloak-and-dagger bit?"

Gene furrowed his brow for a moment. "I'm not looking for cloak-and-dagger. I just want to buy enough time to get some answers and put a stop to whatever is making people sick. But Mary Catherine—I don't know what kind of wasp nest we might be kicking at here."

"Nice image." My stomach knotted.

Gene gently but firmly grasped me by my upper arms. "I'm not kidding. If what our coffee shop friend said is true..."

I picked up where he trailed off, "Then Walkerville wasps carry some pretty wicked stingers."

Gene nodded. "I'm willing to give it all to find the truth. I'm not sure I want you to."

He was right. This wasn't picking up rocks in Quaker Creek and looking for water pennies. This was digging up what two potentially deadly forces—Big Pharma and The Mob—wanted kept buried.

I forced myself to look directly into his eyes. "Search softly," I said, "and poke with a big stick."

***

Since we couldn't sit together, we agreed to divide the workload. First he wanted to be the one to search for anything pertinent on the history of HBC Pharmaceuticals in Walkerville.

I shook my head. "You're the one with medical knowledge. You should be looking up what all our 'curse' sicknesses have in common."

"I already have a lead on that," he said. "Something seems to be making our immune responses dysfunctional."

"Something like dioxin?"

His eyes widened behind his glasses.

"My best friend is a chemistry professor," I explained. "She's been texting me help."

"You know that jam jar of creek water I was holding during the viewing?"

I nodded, realization dawning. "You were collecting samples."

"I have some soil ones, too, but I don't know where to send them—nowhere I know I can trust with the results."

I slid my phone from my purse and typed to Staz: *If I have soil and water samples, can you find someplace near here where we can test them—someone you would trust with our lives?*

"Last night you weren't interested in any of this," Gene said. If he was trying to hide the hurt in his voice, he was doing a bad job.

I sent the text to Staz then admitted, "What Bobby told me last night, after Turo... it got me wondering."

He scowled. "Dioxin has been shown to cause endometriosis in primates, but I can't imagine dioxin being spread by a pharmaceutical company, especially not one that came to town well after the exposure window."

"Exposure window? Like, when we would've had to have been exposed in order to have all these problems."

Gene nodded. "Maybe I shouldn't be looking up HBC. Maybe I should be looking up Walker Chemical."

"You do that. I'll look up HBC."

My phone buzzed as I sat at one of the free computers. *Trust with your lives? Are you being melodramatic?*

No.

As the Web browser opened, I got Staz's reply. *Man o Manichewitz. You're serious. I'll contact some colleagues in Phila and get back to you.*

Over an hour later, I was still absorbed in reading, searching, and copying notes into an email to myself. My phone remained still. Presumably Staz was still working on her end. It wasn't until I heard a loud grumble permeate the new quiet of the room that I realized the kids had cleared out in search of dinner, leaving Gene and me to ourselves.

"Was that you?" I asked.

"Was what me?" he replied, not even looking up from his screen.

"That stomach growl."

"What? Oh, yeah. I guess it was." He waved me over to his station.

I sent the email to myself and closed all my windows. That was about as much cloak-and-dagger as I could think to manage.

Gene pointed to the page open on his screen. "Walker Chemical worked on military contracts off and on, starting with World War I."

"Really? I had no idea they went back that far."

"They specialized in chemical weapons. Mustard gas."

I felt a chill wash through me. "Gross."

"When the Geneva Convention came along in the 1920s, they switched to developing agricultural products."

"Like insecticides and herbicides?"

Gene turned to me. "Your chemist friend fed you that?"

"She makes a good matzo ball soup, too. What else did you find?"

"Well, they picked up a new military contract at the end of the 1950s."

I thought through my history classes. "That's after Korea but leading into…"

Gene picked up where my voice trailed off. "Vietnam."

I felt my stomach sink. "Orange Crush? And I don't mean the R. E. M. song."

"Agent Orange, and I meant the forest defoliant, a known immune disruptor and cause of birth defects in large doses, and a known cause of acne in lower doses."

Gene brushed a knuckle softly against my scarred cheek. I startled, pressing my own fingers to the trail of tingles his touch had left along my skin. I cleared my throat to break the moment. "But none of our classmates or their kids have birth defects."

Gene looked away. "No, but just about all of us have immune problems. Did you hear what kind of cancer Rocco Cargione has?"

"Non-hodgkins," I replied.

"Lymphoma. That's an immune system cancer. Lupus? An autoimmune disorder. Endometriosis? That has no known cause, but current theories suggest it is, at its core, a dysfunction of the immune system. There's even research that is pointing to an autoimmune basis for autism spectrum disorders."

"Like Jennifer's and Tina's kids have."

Gene nodded.

"Okay," I said, "but how did we, specifically the Class of '87, get all this exposure? None of us was old enough to work at Walker while it was still in business. We were all toddlers when the war ended."

Gene nodded. "If the exposure were through the air or the ground water, then The Curse of '87 would be The Curse of the Greater Walkerville Area."

I rubbed my own eyes. "So it's not a curse. It's just chemistry."

Gene leaned back in his chair and gave a sigh of surrender. "Well, what did you find?"

I elbowed him away from his keyboard and brought up my email.

"That's nice. You're giving a presentation to the Seven Dolors students?"

"What?" I looked at the subject line "Seven Dolors Author Visit Contract" just under the email I'd sent myself. "Oh, yeah. My agent wants me to sign that."

"Aren't you going to?"

"Maybe. If I don't get iced by the mafia first."

I opened up my notes and gestured for Gene to read them while I gave him the rundown. "The Walker Chemical property was lying vacant for almost ten years. The EPA came in around 1978 and did some testing. That resulted in this report, which declared all cleanup had been done safely, and the property posed no immediate hazard to area residents."

Gene pointed to the screen, "But HBC bought the property in 1983 for—a thousand bucks? That seems—"

"Lowballed at best?" I nodded. "It was the third site in as many years HBC had purchased at a hugely discounted rate. The year before, they had just spent the same amount on what would become their Niagara Branch in New York State."

I watched Gene mouth the word "Niagara" twice before he turned to me. "Where in New York State?"

"Curiously close to a place called Love Canal." I pointed to the line in my email where I had typed the words, "Love Canal: dioxin dump."

"I remember hearing the name when we were little," I told Gene as I watched the sickly glow of the computer screen play against the increasing pallor of his face. "Love Canal. I didn't realize what exactly happened until our little research project here came up."

Gene removed his glasses and rubbed his eyes. "I did some reading on it a few months ago in my own research, just going on a hunch."

I read off my notes. "A chemical company dumped in a landfill, then a nice neighborhood and a school were built on top of that. In the years after, the community had a huge rise in kids with birth defects, leukemia, messed-up white blood cell counts. The list goes on and on. It's basically what kickstarted the EPA Superfund for environmental cleanup."

Gene opened his mouth to speak, halted, then said, "Did you learn where else you can find dioxin?"

"My wide behind," I said, patting my bottom right cheek.

"Adipose tissue," he corrected, wincing.

"In other words, fat, much of which is stored—"

"I get it. You're hilarious. Dioxin is a bioaccumulative chemical. If it's in or on the things you ingest, it gets stored in body fat, and it just keeps building up."

I eyed him. "Hence the questions about coconut milk or almond milk at the coffee shop. And, well, lots of people are staying away from soy these days."

Gene nodded. "When we eat animal fat, we ingest all the dioxin they've consumed. If we store that in our fat cells, then we're storing that dioxin at a concentrated level.

The more dioxin-laced pesticide animals eat on their feed, the more dioxin they store in their fat cells. The more animal products we consume, the more dioxin we consume."

"So you're not just vegetarian now," I guessed, "you're vegan—no animal matter of any kind?"

Gene gave me one of his rare sheepish looks. "Every once in a while, I'll treat myself to some organically farmed bacon, but otherwise..."

"I hear you," I said, just as my stomach gave a very badly timed grumble. "The vegan life is growing in appeal with every new page I read."

Gene stretched his arms over his head and yawned. "So, hungry?"

I snickered. "Do I remember reading that Walkerville has a new vegetarian Indian buffet?"

***

Half an hour later, I sat at our little table for two. Gene had piled his plate with soft, fragrant discs of *naan* bread, scoops of curried chickpeas, and tumbling servings of multicolored basmati rice. I halfheartedly poked at something called a *kofta*, which looked like a meatball that might spontaneously combust.

"Have you not tried Indian before?" he asked.

"I have, but it's been a while. I guess I just don't have much of an appetite right now, which is surprising, considering I'm due for—"

Dr. Marcasian, OB/GYN, looked up from his plate, still chewing.

I had almost blurted, "due for my period," but I figured that even a gynecologist wouldn't want to hear about that over dinner. I didn't need to say it, though.

Without batting an eye, Gene said, "Severe premenstrual symptoms are common among women with endometriosis. Irritability? Trouble sleeping? Headaches?"

"I haven't even told you whether or not I have endometriosis," I said, as Gene put another spoonful into his mouth.

He chewed and swallowed again. "Overwhelming cravings for sweets, yeast-risen products, and carbohydrates?"

I looked at the untouched but delicious-looking pile of deep-fried balloon bread on my plate. "Doesn't every woman get that, endo or not?"

"Women who have low progesterone are significantly more likely to crave those nutrients the body would use in the production of the lacking hormone, and to crave those things for a longer period of time. Women with low progesterone are far more likely to have endometriosis."

I sighed, not ready to admit my condition outright, but needing to defend where I was. "My condition has been under treatment for many years now, thank you very much."

"Under treatment," he asked, eyebrows raised, "or masked with yet more chemicals?"

I dropped the spoon I was barely using. "Way to be hostile, Gene."

Gene closed his eyes and shook his head with what I hoped was regret. "I'm not hostile towards you. I'm hostile towards a clueless medical establishment. Were you even offered any options besides The Pill?"

I snorted. "Well, I was told pregnancy would be a cure, but I was fifteen when it started, so that wasn't exactly an option for a college-bound Catholic schoolgirl."

Gene put down his fork and placed his hands in his lap. I could tell he was trying to control his emotions by the slow, calculated way he delivered his next words.

"You've been on The Pill since high school."

"Yeah."

"What does your doctor say about that in the face of your, and forgive the term, increasing age?"

"Nothing."

I watched him swallow, even though his mouth had been empty, then he placed his clenched fists on the table in front of him. "No talk of increased clotting risks? No discussion of the mitogenic effects of estrogen on breast tissue? Did they ever even do any bloodwork?"

"Back in high school or more recently?"

"Either."

"No to both."

I watched Gene's face redden in the dim restaurant lighting. "I realize your treatment choices are nobody's business but yours and your doctor's, but I would like to urge you to consider some alternatives."

"Such as?"

"Bloodwork to monitor your hormone levels. A series of ultrasounds to determine the progress of the disease."

"Why would there be progress? Doesn't The Pill just stop endometriosis all together?"

"No. It masks the symptoms, but it's still there. It may even be growing."

I felt a flush of anger wave over me. "Why didn't anyone ever tell me that?"

"Because 70% of the average gynecologist's income comes from The Pill. Most don't have the integrity to kill the cash cow."

I gave him a dirty look across the table, but he remained unfazed. "Then what do you suggest as an alternative?"

"Look into surgical options, precisely timed in your cycle in order to reduce the chance of recurrence. And get a yearly mammogram."

"I'm not 40 yet."

"I don't care."

I made a scoffing noise and threw my napkin down next to my plate.

Gene was scowling like I'd never seen. His voice grew heated. "You've been dosed with a Group 1 Carcinogen on a regular basis for nearly 25 years, not to mention the ever-growing possibility that you were exposed as a child to some sort of immune-disrupting chemical. I don't care what your doctors haven't told you. I don't care what our culture sells as 'normal' or so-called 'acceptable risk.' These are not risks to be taken lightly, Mary Catherine. I could—you might—"

He closed his eyes and lowered his face. I thought of his sister dying. I thought of his mother getting sick over and over again. I pressed one hand to my lips. With the other, I reached across for his hand. I cursed myself for having accused him of being judgmental about my treatment choices.

"I'm sorry," I said through my fingers.

Gene left his hand in mine but did not grip back. "You didn't do anything intentionally."

I swallowed on a throat gone dry. "That's the problem. I just did what everybody else did."

"Of course you did. You were just a kid. Let me guess: Doctor McGinley said it was the most common treatment?"

I remembered that day my mom had brought me into Dr. McGinley's office, wondering if the sudden, thorough pain I'd been having was from kidney stones. "He told us that it was totally safe, totally normal, that there were no risks to worry about."

"Just what he told my sister. Probably what he told the rest of Walkerville, for that matter."

Gene and I looked down at our plates. It seemed we had both lost our appetites. I gestured toward my cooling heap of balloon bread. "If we keep this up, I'll be back into a size seven in no time."

Gene gave me another dreadful look.

"Great," I replied. "Now what?"

"Remember what we said about dioxin storage in—"

"My wide behind?"

"In the adipose tissue of animals."

"How could I forget? Go on."

"If you have been exposed to an extraordinarily high level of dioxin, a rapid weight loss program would burn up large amounts of that adipose tissue and send all that highly-concentrated dioxin flowing through your system. The human body was not made to deal with dioxin in any amount, much less that much of it all at one time."

"Sort of like a poison cattle herd on stampede through the canyons of my bloodstream?"

Gene gave a startled little laugh. "I would have put it far more clinically, but yes, that's somewhat accurate."

I looked down into my lap and couldn't help but notice the width of my thighs. Gene might not have known whether or not he was married, but I was starting to think that I'd be staying single for a long, long time. "So you're saying that for the sake of my health, I should hold on to my adipose tissue?"

Gene winced again. "If you want to reach a healthy body mass index, that's commendable, but be careful about it. Go slowly. Give your liver lots of time to get rid of whatever toxins you may be dealing with."

Then he looked across the table at me, his lips in a firm line. "And I'm saying your behind is just fine the way it is."

"More water?"

We startled and looked up into the face of our waiter,

standing by our side with a sweating plastic pitcher. We pulled our hands away from each other and both mumbled affirmative noises in the waiter's direction. As I listened to the gurgle of my glass being filled, I watched Gene's hands slide even further away from mine.

Unbidden, another memory flew into my mind, of the eighth grade retreat, of standing with Gene in the snow outside the retreat hall kitchen. The square of light from the window falling on the snow that separated our feet. My reaching for Gene's hands. Him reaching back. Him blinking at me in the shadows and the cold. Him dropping my hand and turning away.

"We should probably figure out what we do next."

I blinked out of my reverie and found myself back at the table with an adult Gene. "What?"

He was unrolling his shirtsleeves and rebuttoning them. "What other information do we need in order to bring a case to the authorities?"

I bit on my lower lip and tried to refocus. "Which authorities? Ros—"

"—our friend—"

"Sorry, 'our friend' implied that we might not have any authorities to go to."

"The Love Canal activists went to the EPA. They have an anonymous tip page."

"There's no such thing as an 'anonymous' tip page. They can track our IP address."

"That's right. That's how Alexander McSomething was able to catch Shelbert Welbert when he kidnapped Professor Bhutt-Faix in *Alexander McSomething and the Laundry Room Vortex*."

"Wow. You really did read Alex."

Again, I was treated to another rare sheepish-Gene look. "Like I said, I'm a fan."

"Well, if we get out of this alive and with some justice served up, then I'll send you an autographed copy. Sound good?"

"Don't send it. Bring it to me when you come to my office for a consult."

I froze, caught out.

"I'm sorry. Was that too forward of me?"

"No!" I said. "Well, yes, but I'm starting to see your point on a lot of these matters, the deeper we dig into the dioxin well, so to speak."

He reached into his shirt pocket and passed me a business card. "You would have to call my office, and they'll send you a bloodwork series to get done in advance of the appointment. You'd also need to learn how to chart your cycle so we can determine—"

"Easy there, Trigger." I ran my thumb over the raised ink on the business card. "One step at a time. That might all be well and good for your hard-core Catholic patients—"

He raised his eyebrows. "And what are those, exactly?"

"The ones who have a problem with The Pill, but I'm not one of those. In fact, in case you didn't notice at this morning's funeral, I'm quite fallen away. Anyway, we still have work to do here. Waiter? Separate checks, please?"

We walked back to our cars in what felt to me like an awkward but hopeful silence, which Gene was the first to break. "Have you heard from your chemist friend?"

I took my phone from my purse. There was a text from Staz. *Call this number. It's a colleague of my graduate advisor. She should be able to help you out. Her lab is at Penn. Call there around lunch time tomorrow. She's a late riser.*

"Typical chemist," Gene said, reading over my shoulder.

I gave him a questioning look as we made our way into

the municipal parking lot around the corner from the buffet.

"Sorry," he answered. "There's a rivalry. My undergrad was in physics."

I laughed. "Staz, my best friend the chemist? She says physics is for—"

"Gene! Mary Catherine!"

Gene and I wheeled around and found ourselves facing Bobby Campobello, wearing not his uniform but a striped gray golf shirt. My palm was already sweating as I slid my phone back into my purse.

"Bobby," Gene said. "How are you holding up?"

Bobby nodded. He shuffled into step with us. I smelled alcohol and maybe something less legal on his breath. "I'm good, good. Did you hear? The funeral?"

Gene was eyeing Bobby with much distrust. "Something from this morning, or did you mean for Turo?"

"The one for Turo, my cousin. It's going to be Monday morning at the church. The family's asking for no viewing."

I hugged my arms around myself with the chill and felt Gene step closer to me.

"That's understandable," he said.

"You'll be sticking around for it?" Bobby asked Gene in a slurred voice.

Gene stopped, and we stopped with him. He put his hands in his pockets and rocked back on his heels. "I'll have to make some calls back to the hospital, but I should be there."

Something anxious flickered across Bobby's inebriated face. For a very strange second, his face seemed to droop slightly, too, just as Mrs. Marcasian's face now did.

"Good, good," Bobby said. "And I know Mary Catherine will still be around."

I bit the inside of my cheek, remembering our time in the police station—had it only been the previous night? Then his eyes had been so warmly determined. Now he looked dazed beyond grief, maybe even drugged. It even looked like half of his face was drooping down to his neck.

I had to ask. "Bobby, are you okay? Do you need a ride anywhere?"

His one eye widened—the other responded only weakly. "Really? You'd—? Wait, no, it's not the right time. Not yet."

"Not yet?" Gene repeated. He stepped even closer to me, his arm now against my shoulder. "What do you mean?"

Bobby chuckled to himself. "Sorry, bro. Sorry. I'm just having a hard time. Not making—not making much sense. It's been a rough few days for me."

He hung his head and rubbed the back of his neck with a tanned hand. He was making me nervous, but I still had to ask, "Are you sure? Can you make it home okay?"

"Yeah, I just live up the hill." He gestured in a direction past the parking lot. "I can walk. See you around."

In silence, Gene and I watched him stumble out of the parking lot and around the corner.

"What do you think that was about?" I asked in a whisper.

"I don't know," Gene answered. "I have a feeling we'll find out before Turo's in the ground."

"Yeah." I shuddered. "Great."

Gene drew in a slow breath through his nose. "In the meantime, can we plan for tomorrow?"

I looked at the dark street down which Bobby had recently disappeared. "A plan. Plans are good."

"Even if it means going to the principal's office?"

"The principal's—?"

"I was going to visit Sister Thomas Marie's office to take a look at her records, to see if there's any reason why Rosa would think she was murdered."

I gave him my incredulous face. "What were you going to do? Just breeze on in there and start hacking away at her computer?"

He shrugged a little. "I have carte blanche."

"And how did you acquire this carte blanche?"

"I'm on their board of directors."

"Their board of—Gene, why? I thought we both wanted to leave Seven Dolors behind us?"

He looked down at his feet. "A lot changed when my sister died."

"Gene." I put my hand, still shaking from our strange encounter with Bobby, on his arm. "No matter what you did or didn't do—"

"No."

"—you couldn't have—"

"NO!"

His shout took me with such force that I pulled back my hand and pressed it to my heart.

"No," he said more softly, like a prayer. "I can't change the past. You're right. But I can reach out to kids—kids like she was—"

He looked at me through lowered lids. "Kids like we were. You write for misfits..."

"And you want to protect them," I finished.

He paused, nodded just so slightly, then gave me a smug smile. "Besides, you could use a printer."

"I could?"

"That's right. Don't you have an author visit contract to print out?"

I texted Staz that night, letting her know that I had lots to tell her but no energy with which to do so. I called her first thing the next morning.

"So." I could hear her eating on the other end. "He's not sure if he's married or not, he's trying to get you to be Miss Crunchy Granola Catholic, he's got a great right hook, and he's leading you into mortal danger?"

"Yeah." I sipped my bland hotel room coffee. "Sounds like a real keeper."

"Sounds kind of hot, if you ask me. The last time Geoff got me into anything close to mortal danger was taking me to his parents' house the day his dad was installing a rain barrel."

"Was that when they had to call the fire department?"

"Sadly."

"At least your man is a Krav Maga expert. That and he married you."

"Please. Krav Maga is just something to make him feel big. It's not like he'll ever need to use it or anything. Hey, can I have a theory here?"

"Sure, but don't theorize too long. I have to meet Gene at the school in half an hour, and I still have to do my hair."

"So HBC has all these branches on old toxic waste sites, right?"

"It seems that way. Love Canal, Walkerville, and two in New Jersey."

"Like I said, toxic waste sites."

"Har har. Go on."

"It's obvious they're picking these places deliberately."

"Probably because they're cheap. Who in their right minds would build on sludge piles?"

"I was thinking because they're good investments."

I lowered myself onto the edge of the hotel bed. "What do you mean? Good financial investments?"

"More than that. They'd be good community investments."

I nearly spit out the sip of coffee I'd just taken. "You're suggesting that a big pharmaceutical company is warm and fuzzy and cares about the good of mankind?"

"Hey! As a scientist who actually does aim for the greater good—"

"You majored in chemistry so you could improve the longevity of nail polish."

"Shut up. I'm talking." She paused. "Oy. Pregnant brain. What was I saying?"

"That HBC picks dump sites because they're good investments in humanity."

"Right. That. If HBC is leaking environmental poisons into the area and making people sick, they get themselves a handy nearby population for clinical trials, thereby saving travel expenses. They also get a population who would—"

"—who would rather die than have the government run their free drugs out of town?"

"Free drugs. Free hope. Not to mention jobs and a backbone for the local economy."

"Hmn." I wandered into the bathroom and dug out my toiletry bag. "So you think they're on top of the dump so they can keep it quiet and profitable."

"And they're betting that their test population wouldn't rat on them, even if they got found out." I heard her take another crunch of corn flakes. "Maybe. Like I said, I just have theories. And that list of illnesses you fired off? HBC has a drug line for each. In fact, according to an article in last month's *Business Breakthrough Weekly* they're steadily increasing their share in the hormonal birth control market."

"You're so cute when you're Googling."

"Girl, I'm always cute. Oh! That reminds me."

"Of?"

"Gene. Did he mean 'just fine' as in, 'just fine,' or did he mean, '*juuuuuust fiiiiiine*?'"

***

I stood on the steps to the school's main entrance, waiting for Gene. I was dressed and sweating in my last clean piece of businesslike attire, given I had been expecting to be back on the road and home no later than that morning. I checked my watch. 9:06, which meant Gene was uncharacteristically late. School was supposed to have started at 8:15, but the building was curiously quiet. It was Friday in late May. I ran down a spotty mental list of Holy Days of Obligation, and could only think of Ascension Thursday as a possible reason for the school to be closed. Maybe that had been yesterday, and the school just made it a four-day weekend? In that case, Gene would have to have either a key to the whole building or another plan.

Then I remembered that Sister's funeral had been yesterday, and a funeral could not have been held on a Holy Day. Man, I really was fallen away if I had forgotten that. Just as I pulled up the Web browser on my phone to see if I could find the calendar for Our Lady of the Seven Dolors Catholic Elementary School, the doors of the church across the street opened. Uniformed school children, herded by their teachers, came trickling out. Ah, yes. Friday morning Mass. Sister Thomas Marie had made that a weekly institution during our last year, shortly after the death of Tony Vitale.

I held a hand out over my eyes as a shield against the bright morning sun, and I looked around for Gene. I saw him, exiting the church at a door to my left. I noticed the older children stopping to wave hello to him, some of the younger ones giving him high-fives. All the teachers who passed him nodded and gave him warm smiles. Gene smiled back at each in turn, but his warmest smiles, the ones that made his whole face light up, he gave to the children. I even heard several of them calling him, "Dr. M."

I hopped down from the steps to the school and prepared to cross the street to meet him. As I did so, though, someone made me wish I had stayed where I'd been.

"*Catarina, bella!*"

"Oh. Hi, Mr. Celli."

Mr. Celli was wearing a blood-red Hawaiian shirt covered with a sailboat print, green polyester shorts, and, yes, brown socks with black sandals. He doffed his white straw fedora to peck me on the cheek. A car coming down the street honked at us to get out of the way.

"*Cafone!*" Mr. Celli shouted back. "Don't you see these little angels crossing the street?"

I grabbed Mr. Celli by the elbow and steered him back to the safety of the sidewalk. Gene stood by the door he'd just exited, uniformed children streaming past him.

"Mr. Celli, do you remember my friend Gene from grade school? Gene, this is Mr. Celli."

"Your neighbor, I remember." Gene held out his hand. "Good to see you again, sir."

Mr. Celli's eyes lit with recognition. "I saw you in Mass this morning! Good boy, good boy."

Gene put his hands in his pockets and looked awkward. "Thank you, sir."

Mr. Celli leaned in toward Gene conspiratorially. "You go every day?"

Gene glanced at me and the color rose in his cheeks. "When I'm not delivering babies, yes, sir, I do."

"Ah, God bless! So," Mr. Celli asked, eyeing us each in turn, "You two staying in town for the DiFrancesco boy's funeral, eh?"

"Yes, sir," Gene said.

Mr. Celli grunted. "*Cafone*, that boy, and the son of a *putana*."

I giggled uneasily. "I don't remember what either of those words mean, but I do remember they're bad."

"I think he just speculated on Turo's mom's profession," Gene mock-whispered in my ear. I hoped he couldn't see my goosebumps.

"Sorry, I know I shouldn't speak ill of the dead." Mr. Celli turned back toward the church and blessed himself.

"It's okay, Mr. Celli," I said. "I kind of know how you feel."

"I wasn't apologizing to you!" Mr. Celli pointed with one thumb behind him at the church, patting his belly with the other. "I was apologizing to Him."

"Oh," I mumbled. "Right."

"Ha! *Bella*! It's okay!" He turned to Gene. "She's a good girl, this one, and I can tell you're a good boy."

I snickered a bit at the thought of a gynecologist being called a "good boy." Gene glared at me, but then Mr. Celli clapped him on the shoulder.

"She's a good girl," he said to Gene, very seriously. "Keep an eye on her, will ya?"

Gene returned with equal gravity, "Yes, sir, Mr. Celli."

"Good boy," Mr. Celli said. Then he replaced his white fedora atop his head and shuffled back down to the parking lot.

After watching him go, Gene and I simultaneously sighed then turned to each other.

Scratching awkwardly at the back of my neck, I asked, "Off to the principal's office with us then?"

Gene beckoned me to follow him across the street. "Sure. Like Mr. Celli said, somebody's got to keep an eye on you. Do you have your jump drive?"

"In other words, do I have our cover story?" I took my key ring out of my purse and dangled it between us. My jump drive, cased in pale blue plastic, caught the light like a piece of stained glass. "Do you have something for the samples?"

He patted his side pocket. "Just a few swab vials. I'm hoping your friend's colleague will have the equipment to analyze whatever it is we're able to scrape up."

As we climbed the four stairs into the school, I noticed that the crowds of children heading in through the side entrances were far more subdued than I would have expected them to have been. Gene held the door open for me, and we turned right, making our way towards the main office. I recognized a portrait hanging in the hallway. The subject had same blue eyes as Tony Vitale had had, but this face was softly aged, and his light brown hair held sharp streaks of gray.

2008 DISTINGUISHED ALUMNUS AWARD
CHRISTOPHER J. VITALE, MBA, PharmD, PhD
OUR LADY OF THE SEVEN DOLORS
ELEMENTARY SCHOOL
CLASS OF 1984

Again, our late classmate's brother, Chris. I didn't remember seeing all this alphabet soup after his name on the Birnam Wood-sized floral arrangement at Sister's viewing.

"Looks like someone has done well for himself," I said

to Gene, indicating the portrait. Gene gave icy silence for a response and, with one hand lightly resting on the small of my back, steered me into the main office.

"Mrs. Reale?" I nearly shrieked as we stepped inside. Mrs. Margaret Reale had been the secretary here since our third grade year.

"Mary Catherine Whelihan, is that you?" She stood up from her chair and nearly knocked it over in her haste to hug me.

I accepted her embrace happily. "And I'm not even asking you to send me home sick this time."

Mrs. Reale giggled. "I always wondered if you spent so much time in this office because you were really sick, or were you just—"

"Sick of this place? A little from Column A, a little from Column B," I admitted.

"And I see you've brought our favorite doctor with you," Mrs. Reale said, turning to Gene and taking his hand in both of hers. I could now see that her wire-rimmed glasses had become bifocals. Her hair was no longer its former auburn but a bottled version with snow white roots showing at the bottom. She was short and slight of build, but she pounded around her office like a tiny tornado, getting us coffees, papers flying in her wake. She pounded after them to put them back in place, then rushed back to fill our coffees again.

"I'm sorry," she said, passing us mugs that read respectively "World's Best Secretary" and "World's Best Grandmother." "Everything has been topsy-turvy since...well..."

Gene spoke first. "Sister Thomas Marie was the mortar between the bricks of this place. Dolors will never be the same now she's gone."

"And then what happened with Mr. DiFrancesco," Mrs.

Reale said, tilting her head meaningfully at Gene. "The archdiocese is sending in grief counselors and everything, just like after the church fire. I'm not sure how much more of this our little school can take."

"That's right." I nodded as sympathetically as I could. "Turo's children go here. How are they holding up?"

"Oh, it's not just his children. It's the whole school. Didn't you know? Turo DiFrancesco is—was—our head of maintenance."

I turned my eyes to Gene. "Did you know this? You're on their board, after all."

Gene shrugged in wonderment. "No. I was mostly involved in—"

"Dr. M here advises on and provides chastity education for Seven Dolors."

Gene added, "At Sister Thomas Marie's request."

"*Buon'anima.*" Mrs. Reale blessed herself.

"Mrs. Reale," I said, "forgive me for not knowing, but what did Sister die of, anyway? Was she sick for a while?"

She flopped back into her chair and passed her hand over her brow. "Not very, no. I mean, not like cancer or anything. She was getting old, like the rest of us. I retire next year, you know. Anyway, she was hardly ever sick a day she was here, but just like the rest of us, she started breaking down."

Gene and I exchanged a look over her head. He asked, "Breaking down how?"

"Oh, you know, the longer we work with kids, the more they wear on us. Kids aren't like they used to be, you know. Nothing like the superstars you kids were."

I nearly snarfed my coffee out my nose. Gene patted my back.

"Anyway," Mrs. Reale added, "it was right after we got back from Christmas break. We both got a very bad case of bronchitis. It seemed to take forever for us to shake it. I got better a little before Valentine's Day, but Sister never really seemed to improve. She was coughing all the time, but she kept working, working harder if anything else. She was here before I arrived each morning, and I never saw her leave before I did."

"Why do you think she was working so much harder?" I asked.

"I have no idea," she said. "We'd already passed our accreditation the previous year. Christmas insanity was over. We were months away from state testing. I asked her once what she was so busy with. 'Just wrapping some things up,' she said. And she left it at that. A week later she was in the hospital with pneumonia. She never came back."

Mrs. Reale hung her head and reached for the needlepoint box of tissues on her desk. She dabbed her eyes and shook her head a little. "I'm sorry."

"No apology necessary," Gene said softly. I studied his face. He seemed lost in thought.

"Anyway." I watched Mrs. Reale deliberately brighten. "Is there something I can help you with?"

A few minutes later we were ushered into Sister Thomas Marie's office, the door to which was just behind Mrs. Reale's desk.

As soon as the door opened, I said, "It smells different than I remember."

Mrs. Reale rolled her eyes. "I know. It's the stink bug spray. Mr. DiFrancesco started spraying it last Fall, when things got really bad."

"There's a spray for stink bugs?" I asked.

She shrugged. "It doesn't seem to work, but at least it smells better than the critters themselves. Smells a bit like lilies, I think."

I held a knuckle under my nose. "I guess I don't like the smell of lilies."

Mrs. Reale stabbed the computer's power button with a manicured thumb. "You should be able to just log on as a guest."

She said nothing when Gene slid the door shut behind us. As I booted up the computer, Gene pulled the sample vials out of his pocket.

"Do you even know what you're looking for?" I hissed to him.

"Do you?" He was putting on a pair of latex gloves.

I touched the keyboard, and it felt slick, as if it had last been touched by someone who had put on too much moisturizer.

"Well?" Gene demanded.

"I'm looking for any files or notes Sister kept that might reference Walker Chemical, HBC, or toxic chemicals."

He was peering into empty coffee cups one by one. "And I'm searching for any evidence that Sister was poisoned."

"Do you really think Sister would have let herself be taken to the hospital with dirty mugs left in her office?"

"No." He swiped a long-handled swab inside one of the mugs. "But if the poison weren't water-soluble, there might be residue left behind, even now. In fact, do me a favor."

A pair of purple exam gloves landed on the keyboard before me. I held them up between thumb and forefinger. "What will these do? Keep my prints off the keyboard that Mrs. Reale knows I'm using?"

"If it is poison, it might be something absorbed through the skin. No better place for her to come in regular contact with it than her keyboard."

My mouth went dry. I put the gloves on, then I held the

keyboard up to Gene. He ran a swab along several of the keys then sealed the swab in its vial.

I took the keyboard back and waited. At first I was cursing the glacial speed of the nun's technology, but then I thought of something.

"Yes!" I whispered when it actually worked. Within a few seconds, I was in Sister's password-protected email.

Gene was looking over my shoulder as he swiped the handle of the drawer next to my right thigh. "Something you learned researching for Alex?"

"Kind of," I said. "Research done before Alex even came along. It's something I picked up from..."

"From?"

I halted. "My ex-fiancé. It's a long story."

Gene stopped his random swabbing for a minute. "Do you want to talk about it?"

I coughed a laugh. "We'll talk when you know whether or not you're actually married. Anyway, I learned it so long ago, let's just be happy that Catholic schools don't have the funding to update their tech all that often."

"*Deo gratias*, then." He took his last swab over to the radiator along the inside wall.

I returned my attention to the late principal's inbox. "Well, *there's* something to print besides that author contract."

"What did you find?"

"A receipt email from epa.gov dated yesterday. It says they got her message and will forward it on to the proper offices within their agency."

Gene froze then gave me a look over his shoulder. "Is the text from her email to them included?"

"No. You really thought this was going to be that easy?"

I clicked on her "sent mail" folder, but there was a lot in there, mostly to what I guessed were personal email addresses, parents and the like. I did a quick search for the word "dioxin." Nothing. "Walker Chemical." Nothing. "Pharmaceuticals." Nothing.

"Duh," I reprimanded myself. "Search the 'to' field, you doof."

"What?"

"Nothing. Just berating myself."

I typed "epa.gov" into the search field, and there they were: email after email. The first had been sent on January 8 of last year.

"It took them over a year to get back to her," I whispered in disbelief.

Gene was back, reading over my shoulder.

To whom it may concern:

"Pristine grammar," I said offhandedly. "At least she practiced what she preached."

I am principal of Our Lady of the Seven Dolors Catholic Elementary School in Walkerville, PA, just outside Philadelphia. I am writing to request testing of soil, drinking water and groundwater on the campus of our school and in the general area. I have reason to believe that a memorial garden on our campus as well as a building foundation—

"Mrs. Reale," I heard a familiar voice say, muffled through the door that shielded us from him.

"Why Mr. Farzza," Mrs. Reale replied. "We weren't expecting you today."

I quickly closed the email and looked back at Gene. His face did not lose color, but I could see him clenching his jaw.

"Yeah, sorry it took so long to get out here," our classmate told the secretary. "I didn't get a chance to work on Sister's computer until now."

The bottom dropped out of my stomach.

"I'm guessing he's their network guy," Gene whispered in my ear. This time I didn't get goosebumps from the feel of his lips so close to my ear. I already had them from fear of the vendetta-driven bully on the other side of the office door.

Mrs. Reale said, "Would you mind waiting a few minutes? I'm lending her computer to someone who's helping out the school. You remember Mary Catherine Whelihan?"

"What do we do?" I whispered back to Gene.

Mrs. Reale went on. "She was in your class, wasn't she? Have you had a chance to say hello while she's in town?"

Gene leaned away from me and toward the window behind the desk. "We can risk facing him and finding out he's involved in this, or we could run for it."

"She with somebody else?" Frank asked.

"I'm in heels, Gene! And that drop is like six feet."

Mrs. Reale practically sang, "Why yes, another of your classmates, Eugene Marcasian!"

Gene looked back out the window. "Not that far. Only five."

"*Five?*"

"Marcasian, huh? Awesome. I've been wanting to catch up with him since yesterday."

I shot up from the chair. I peeled off my exam gloves and dropped them into the trash can. I kicked off my heels and handed them to Gene. Then I opened the aluminum window and popped out the screen. "You'd better follow me."

The jump wasn't as bad as I'd feared, but it wasn't all that great, either. I thudded down to the narrow strip of grass that framed the building out from the parking lot. Before I could even recover enough to look up, I saw my heels bounce down next to me, followed shortly by a breathless Gene.

"You forgot something." He handed me my purse. Then he peeled his gloves off and dropped them inside. "Is your smartphone still in there?"

I patted around for the form of my phone. "Yeah. Why?"

He took my wrist and pulled me to my feet. "Because eventually we'll need to look up the train schedule down to Penn. We have to cut through the park to the station."

I nodded, whispering back, "If we drive, he'll follow us."

I barely had time to get my feet back into my shoes before Gene was pulling me towards the hill, into the valley, back to the creek that I hadn't visited since I'd found a dead body in it.

CHAPTER THIRTEEN
TAKE MY BREATH AWAY

"Just like old times?" Gene asked. In his rubber-soled business oxfords, Gene picked with relative ease through the creekside brush.

"Oh, sure," I drawled. "A possible mobster on our tail, your pocket full of poison swabs, and me in heels as we walk through mud along the creek where I once found a dead child's body. Yeah, just like old times."

It was hot and humid, and the vegetation above provided little shade so close to the creek bed itself, but I was shivering. Okay, shaking was more accurate. I had not been back to the creek since the time I'd found Tony Vitale. So I really couldn't tell if my difficulty breathing was because I was having some kind of panic attack or because my asthma was kicking up again, just as it had with Bobby at the police station. At least our route wouldn't take us past the railroad bridge, where I'd found Tony.

"At least this time you have a smartphone that gave us the train schedule," he said to me over his shoulder.

I wanted to say, "Thank God for small favors," but all the talking I had just done had sapped my lungs. I tried coughing. When that didn't work so well, I grabbed the skinny trunk of the nearest tree for balance. I tried coughing harder but only wheezed instead.

Gene stopped. He turned to face me, frowning. "You sound bad."

I wiped the sweat from my forehead with the back of my wrist. "Ya think?"

He stepped closer and studied my face. "You're wheezing, but you haven't lost color. Your lips aren't blue."

He took my hand, and he felt me pull back.

He gave me a puzzled look. "I'm going to check your fingernails to see if your circulation is still okay."

I hesitated but nodded and let him look.

He squeezed my nail beds white and watched them go pink again. "Good. We're still early in your distress. Do you have an inhaler with you?"

I jerked my neck back for a deep breath. "No. I haven't had an asthma attack in years, so I stopped carrying it. I think I'm allergic to Walkerville."

He pulled his own phone out of his pocket—an older model, just a phone, not a smart one. I expected a doctor to have all the latest gadgets. Then I thought about his hint that his practice lost money by not prescribing birth control and wondered what other sacrifices he may have made in the name of his beliefs.

"Patty? Hey, it's Gene Marcasian. Can you fax a scrip for me? Thanks. Call it in to the outpatient pharmacy at the University of Pennsylvania. I need an albuterol inhaler for Mary Catherine Whelihan—yeah, I know, not our usual realm of medicine. It's an emergency."

When his call was done, he craned his neck and looked around us in all directions. "I was going to have you lean against a tree. It looks like this one is the most stable around."

"Lean?"

Gene nodded. "Put your purse down, face this tree and press against it with your arms as straight as you can get them. I'd rather get you to an emergency room just to get you on a nebulizer, but percussion will do for now."

"What's percussion?"

"I appreciate your curiosity, but you're wasting valuable time that you could be using to escape on a train."

I gave him a dirty look before following doctor's orders.

Then Gene was thumping on my back with his hands. "Is this okay?"

I nodded. After a few minutes, my lungs still felt tight, and phlegm was juicing up every breath I took, but I felt like I was able to speak again. "Interesting skill set for a gynecologist to have."

"It's something I picked up on my pulmonary medicine rotation during med school."

"Is that where you picked up your maybe-ex-wife?"

I instantly regretted saying that.

Gene's hands slowed down but picked back up again. "No. She was long gone by third year of med school."

I did the math in my head. "You were divorced by the time you were 25?"

"I was divorced before I finished undergrad."

I flipped around to face him, and he held his cupped hands frozen in the air between us. "How old were you when you got married?"

"Frances died in the Winter of my junior year at Penn. Alisha told me she was pregnant that summer. We got married right before school started again in August."

He was completely expressionless in the telling. He let his hands fall to his sides.

"That's it?" I asked.

"That's it."

"Did she divorce you because you're always this cold and clinical about the women you touch?"

I probably should have regretted saying that, but seeing the color finally flare in Gene's face was particularly gratifying. That is, until the words he said next.

"I was going through a rough time when I met Alisha. My parents were divorcing. My sister was on drugs, and I don't just mean The Pill. I had made myself a promise seven years before that I would be someone's hero and wait until I got married to have sex."

Seven years? "You were keeping a promise you'd made when you were fourteen?"

"When we were in eighth grade," he replied with the calm of a rock. "At the retreat."

"At the..." In my mind I was reaching for his hands in the snow outside the retreat building. He had reached for me and pulled away. "Right after the chastity talk," I filled in.

"What can I say? I'm a nerd. I was listening."

Hadn't I been listening? I had tried to stay a virgin, but when senior year of high school came along, and I was the only one of my friends who still was, and Sean Chambers finally asked me to the prom, and I was already on The Pill, so...

Gene broke through my thoughts. "Alisha caught me at a bad time. I made a bad decision. Everything I'd been holding on to—my family, my faith—seemed to have lost its meaning. So I let myself lose meaning with someone who had already forgotten hers."

He stepped back from me and turned his face away.

"That summer, she emailed me to tell me she was pregnant."

"She told you she was pregnant over email!"

Gene gave a short, bitter laugh through his nose. "All I'd given her was my email address. It was a novelty at the time. In fact, hers was one of the first emails I ever received. She asked me for 'help,' and that's when she did give me her phone number."

I could tell by the weight in his voice that there was far more to be said. "What kind of 'help' did she ask you to give? Was she asking you to marry her?"

"No. She wanted me to pay for an abortion."

I swallowed hard. While I was pro-choice myself, I

could never bring myself to do such a thing. Less so could I imagine Gene paying for the death of his own child. "So you asked her to marry you instead."

Gene nodded. "The week after we moved in together, the week before school started back up again, she told another guy he was the father."

"And?"

"He gave her what I wouldn't."

I remembered Gene's choking up at the pub when he said the word "children." I thought of his outreach to the current students at Dolors. Not only did it make sense to my clueless eyes, but it gained a cruel weight, this reality of his life.

I twisted for a good breath then asked, "Do you know if it was yours?"

"If by 'it' you mean the baby?" He turned angry eyes back to me. "I don't know. Alisha was pretty normal."

"And what do you mean by 'normal'?"

"Sex first, relationship later. That's what contraception does to the mind and heart. Sex isn't about connecting with someone on an eternal level anymore. It's just scratching an itch."

He gave me a look as if he wanted me to say something about that summary, but I couldn't. "So you and Alisha—"

"We were only together the one time before she sent that email. She told me later that she was with several other guys around the time she would have conceived."

"Gene," I said quietly. "Bobby said he has no sperm count. Even you're pretty confident that Turo had to use IVF. There's every chance that—"

"—that I'm infertile, too. I know. I've considered that."

"But you don't know? Don't you have ways of finding out?"

He shrugged and looked away into the woods ahead of

us. "Yes, but there hasn't been a need. I haven't even dated since Alisha."

"That sounds lonely."

He nodded. "It is."

"Gene, I may be fallen away, but I did take twelfth grade theology at Cardinal Neumann High." I paused to cough twice, and both coughs actually made me feel better. "Even I know that, if anyone has grounds for an annulment, it's you."

"Here's hoping that the archdiocesan marriage tribunal agrees." Gene gave the space between us a sarcastic grimace. "If they can ever find Alisha to get her testimony. That's why it's been held up. Nobody can find her."

I shook my head. "Why can't the stupid Church make an exception to their antiquated rules? Can't they just set you free? Isn't it just a piece of paper?"

Gene turned disbelieving eyes on me. "You don't get it, do you?"

I opened my arms out to the space around us. "Get what?"

"The Church is the only woman I have in my life right now. She doesn't change Her mind about me. She's let me bring children into the world instead of taking them away from me, and She values my gifts and integrity for what they are. Why would I want Her to change?"

The passionate determination in his eyes at that moment was something I'd never seen in any man before in my entire life. At first I was angry, resentful that he would love an organization so much that he wouldn't even give me a chance in the here and now. But as he kept up our stare-down, I was the first to look away. I was ashamed that I didn't have anything in my life to which I was so dedicated, not even my writing. I then saw that I was developing a grudging admiration of his stoic devotion to something so much bigger than himself.

Just after I looked back down and coughed again, Gene asked, "Are you feeling better now?"

I looked up and gave him a nod. "Just go slowly?"

He gestured for me to go first. I didn't need him to lead. It had been a while, but we both knew the way.

After a few minutes, I spoke over the soft crunching of our shoes against the scrubby creek bank vegetation. "Gene?"

"What?"

"I may have been on The Pill for most of my life. I may not be pure as the driven snow. I may be fallen away—"

"So you've said."

"But," and here I paused and looked over my shoulder to meet his eyes. "If you're holding me up to Alisha's standards, I'm not all that 'normal.'"

Gene stopped. He looked up from the path and gave me a reluctant smile.

"Good to know," he said.

***

We made it to the part of Philadelphia called University City by mid-afternoon. We arrived hungry, scratched and dirty, but we seemed to have shaken Frank or anyone else who might have followed us. I called the number that Staz had given us, and Dr. PJ Heckler gave us directions to her lab. I told her we'd be there in about an hour.

"An hour?" Gene asked after I'd hung up. "The pharmacy is right up 34th Street. We don't need an hour to go get your inhaler."

I sighed. "I'm a flesh and blood woman, Gene. I'm thirsty, I'm hungry, and I need new shoes."

It was a whole new brand of weird doing such mundane things with Gene: going to the pharmacy, having lunch (Gene was pleased to see that his favorite vegetarian

Middle Eastern food truck was still in business) then going shopping with him in tow. More than once, as I picked out a pair of espadrilles and tried on components for a new outfit, I found Gene waiting for me like all the other boyfriends and husbands I'd seen at clothes stores, waiting for their women. The phrase "old married couple" kept coming to mind.

"I needed more clothes anyway," I explained to Gene as I pulled the tags off of the aqua cotton blouse I'd just purchased. "I didn't pack for a stay this long. I'll still have to go to the Laundromat, but at least this buys me a day."

"You could do your laundry at my mom's place."

I stopped short, taken aback. "You don't think she'd mind? Showing up with dirty laundry seems a bit uncouth, even for me."

He smiled. "She won't care. I bet she even bought a box of microwave popcorn for you after she saw you at the library."

Fed, clothed, and medicated as necessary, we arrived at the door plated "P. J. HECKLER, PhD, ENVIRONMENTAL CHEMISTRY." Other than a slightly different shape and a lack of windows, Dr. Heckler's lab looked disturbingly similar to Staz's. Lots of fluorescent light, lots of equipment of varying sizes cluttering up walkways and counters, lots of white walls tacked up with charts and graphs and cat macros printed off of the internet. White-coated, ponytailed, soul-patched minions were off by a bay of empty glass cages, removing Chinese food cartons from a cart.

"Are you Cate?" asked a woman with close-cropped brown hair and olive skin. She did not look that much older than her minions.

I moved forward to shake her hand. "Dr. Heckler? It's great to meet you. Thanks so much for agreeing to—HOLY RATS!"

Both Gene and Dr. Heckler burst out laughing as I leapt back from the aforementioned minions, one of whom was now removing a large, brown-spotted rat from a Chinese container.

"That's how they transport rats between labs," Gene explained once his apoplectic laughter subsided. "That way nobody sees rats being carried around campus and freaks out like you just did. They just see lab geeks with Chinese food."

I pressed my hands to my eyes. "Staz is going pee herself when she hears about this."

Dr. Heckler thumped her chest right below her clavicle, and that seemed to have the effect of halting her laughter. "Your secret is safe with me. And you must be Dr. Marcasian."

Gene shook her hand as well. "Yes, thanks for meeting with us."

"So Dr. Greenfield-Molinsky said you had some samples for me?"

Gene pulled the cluster of swab vials from his pockets. "I had soil and creek water as well, but we got sidetracked from picking them up on our way here."

I felt my phone buzzing in my purse. Someone was calling me. It could wait.

Dr. Heckler took the vials and transferred them over to the nearest lab bench. She looked doubtful. "There's not much here."

"Well," I said, "we didn't have time to get much before we had to jump out a window."

Dr. Heckler raised an eyebrow at me but didn't ask for more. "I'll take what we can get and see what I can do. What exactly am I looking for, anyway?"

Heart still pounding from the unexpected rat sighting, I looked up at Gene. "Just dioxin?"

Gene frowned. "I'm not sure. Dioxin? Pharmaceutical chemicals? Something we haven't imagined yet. Anyway, we need some information stat—before anyone knows we're even looking for it."

Dr. Heckler made thoughtful clicking noises with her tongue. "You're lucky I owe Greenfield-Molinsky's old advisor a bunch of favors. Dr. Breen?"

The sole female minion looked up from her Chinese rat tote.

"Take these and let's get started." Dr. Heckler turned back to us. "I have Cate's number. I'll call you when I have anything."

"When will that be?" I asked.

She shook her head and gave us a grimacing smile. "I'm not sure, but I'll call you as soon as I have some answers for you."

During the walk back to the train, I pulled out my phone and checked the caller ID. It was a number with a southeastern Pennsylvania area code, but the rest of it I didn't recognize. Whoever it was had left a voicemail. Just as I was about to check it, I got a text from Staz.

Any luck with Heckler yet? Call me l8r. Geoff @ Krav Maga awards banquet, will be home late again=lonely preggo.

I replied, *Dr. Heckler will do her best with what little we could give her. I'll fill in the deets when I call you tonight. Off to G's mom's place to do my laundry.*

As we descended the steps down to the train platform, Gene asked me, "How are you feeling? You seem to be breathing better."

"I am, thanks. I'm glad you were here. It's been so long since I've taken an inhaler that I kind of forgot how. Apparently that isn't like riding a bike."

I dialed up my voice mail and plugged in my password.

"Good afternoon Mrs. Whelihan—-"

"I'm a 'Miss,'" I muttered at the male voice, but as I listened to the rest of the message, I stopped walking. I couldn't move my legs any further because they had become jelly.

Gene saw my face and asked, "What is it?"

I held up a hand while I committed the return number to memory. As I waited for my call to ring through, I told Gene, "It's the hotel. They said someone's broken into my room."

CHAPTER FOURTEEN
TAKE ON ME

I stood in the doorway of my hotel room, looking at the chaos. Everything had been turned upside down and inside out. The pillows had been disemboweled. The mattress had been ripped up. The safe had been pulled out of the closet wall and opened, revealing itself to be as empty as I had left it. The smoke alarm dangled by a wire from the ceiling. Light fixtures were smashed. My suitcase had been cut open, my clothes tossed about. Even the curtains lay in shreds upon the floor.

Behind my right shoulder stood Bobby Campobello, sober again and in uniform. His voice was soft, apologetic. "Sorry, Mary Catherine. You'll have to go in and see if anything's been stolen."

I took another step forward and peered inside the bathroom. My makeup case had been spilled on the bathroom floor, the bottles and compacts cracked and spilled.

A warm hand gently grasped my left shoulder. It was Gene. "Are you okay?" he asked for the thousandth time since we had been on the train.

I could only manage a tiny rabbit nod. My rosewater perfume bottle lay shattered on the bathroom floor. The smell that I usually loved was nauseating.

A crime scene photographer was shouldering his way past me, Bobby and Gene into the room, immediately followed by someone who broke out the fingerprint dusting powder.

"Mary Catherine?"

"Yes," I replied to Bobby. My voice sounded as if it were floating somewhere over my head, not coming from my constricted throat.

"I said, do you think anything was stolen?"

My wallet and my phone had been in my purse. I made a quick mental inventory of what I'd left behind in my room: just clothes, shoes, and makeup...and—

"My laptop," I said. "Is it here?"

"We'll have to wait for the photographer to finish—"

"Ew," said the photographer, just before snapping a picture. "Did you mean this laptop?"

I looked down on the floor to the spot he indicated. I squeaked in agony. There was my laptop, all right. The screen had been broken off then snapped in two. The keyboard looked as if it had been smashed with a sledgehammer.

Gene put his hands on my shoulders. "Are you—?"

"I'm just fabulous, thanks for asking," I snapped.

Bobby scratched the back of his neck and sighed. "Did you have anything important on there?"

"Just notes for my next book, but I've barely even started, and what little was there, I hate. I don't have many good work habits, but I do generally save important things on my thumb drive rather than on the laptop itself."

"So whoever it was didn't find what they were looking for," Gene said, letting his hands slip off my shoulders.

"What do you think they might have been looking for, anyway?" Bobby asked.

I felt Gene's eyes on me, but I immediately thought of Rosa's warning about talking to Bobby. I shook my head.

Gene asked, "Were any other rooms broken into?"

Bobby shook his head. "Just Mary Catherine's."

"Why is this happening to me?" I whispered.

Bobby sighed and leaned against the door post. "Turo's note, and now this? I was really hoping you could tell me. Where were you when all this happened, anyway?"

"Um, I was with Gene."

"We went into the city." Gene held up the shopping bag he'd been carrying for me. "We had lunch. She went shopping."

Bobby's mouth went tight. "You two patch things up, I guess?"

Gene stepped to my side and addressed my profile. "Patch up what?"

"I told Bobby about the fight we had at Bep's my first night here."

Gene made his face blank. "Oh. How did that come up?"

Bobby looked from me then to Gene, then back to me again. He was still looking at me as he answered Gene's question. "I was asking her some questions the night of Sister's viewing, the night of Chernobyl."

Gene and I looked at Bobby, both of us completely confused. Both of us asked simultaneously, "Chernobyl?"

"Did you mean Turo?" I asked. I turned to Gene. "Bobby showed me his suicide note at the station."

Gene's jaw tightened. "You'll have to fill me in later."

"Bobby." I was eager to change the subject. "I really don't think I had anything stolen. Destroyed, yes. Stolen, no."

"Can you think of who might have done this," Bobby asked, "anybody who might want something from you?"

I thought of something that might have a kernel of truth to it but still throw Bobby off, if Rosa were right about him. "The only person who ever bothered me since grade school was Sean Chambers."

Gene's eyebrows went up, but Bobby did not look surprised. Still, Bobby was the one to ask, "Who's that?"

"My ex-boyfriend from high school, but he hasn't tried to contact me in over fifteen years. We had a bad breakup. He stalked me for a while, then I scared him off."

"How?" Bobby asked.

I tilted my head, uncomfortable with the admission I was about to make. "Among other things, I bought a gun."

Bobby nodded, but Gene stepped back in shock.

"I never even learned how to use the thing," I admitted. "I was so frightened just owning it that I returned it three days later and signed up for a self-defense seminar instead."

"I knew," Bobby said.

I felt my jaw drop. Gene stared at Bobby, asking, "How?"

Bobby sighed. "The mention of Mary Catherine on Turo's suicide note has thrown up some red flags. We've had to do some investigating into her background, and—"

His phone rang. He took it from his pocket and read the ID. "It's the station."

I glanced at the two-way radio on his other hip and formed the mental question, "Why aren't they using the radio?" Bobby stepped away to take the call faster than I could ask.

I leaned toward Gene. "I think I'm under suspicion in Turo's death."

Gene's eyes narrowed behind his glasses. "That's impossible."

"Nothing is impossible. Bobby just got me to rat myself out on past gun ownership."

His shoulders stiffened at the repeated mention of me ever owning a gun. "That in and of itself is not a crime."

"I was mentioned in the suicide note, and I don't have any alibi for the time of his death but you and the trees behind the church. Both of us were bullied by him. We both have motivation to want the guy dead. You might be pulled in as an accomplice."

Gene dropped his shoulders and took mine gently in his

hands. "Mary Catherine, I think you're getting a little bit paranoid."

"Oh really, Mr. Big Pharma Conspiracy?"

Gene opened his mouth to answer, but his phone rang. He pulled it from his pocket and answered. "Hi, Mom."

I could not hear what Mrs. Marcasian was saying on the other end, but I could hear her panicked tone. I watched Gene's face go paler. When she paused, he asked, "Did you already call the police?"

More anxiety from her end.

"I'll be right there." He hung up. I saw a tremor in his hand. "Someone broke into my mom's apartment while she was at work. I think I know what they took."

***

Bobby seemed reluctant to let me get in Gene's car, asking three times if I wanted to ride in the squad car with him instead. He let me have my way.

"But I'm tailing you," he said, "just in case."

Gene acknowledged this with a grunt, and we took off for his car.

"This ride is going to be short." Gene turned the ignition. "We have to talk and quickly."

I clipped my seatbelt into place just before Gene hit the accelerator, jolting me forward and back. "What do you think they took?"

"The soil and water samples. The only two places that have been broken into are yours and mine. The one thing that ties those two places together is our investigation. Who is the one person who knows for sure that we're working together on something and hiding it?"

"Frank Farzza." I braced myself as Gene sped around a corner. "And he wants vengeance on you for knocking him out in front of the whole class."

Gene nodded. "So we can assume Frank is not an ally."

"Can we assume Rosa is?"

Gene hesitated, twisting his fingers around the steering wheel. "We can only hope so. She even offered us a clue."

"That she seems to be the only one who's escaped The Curse of '87. Oh! And we have another clue, too."

"Which is?"

"Sister's email to the EPA. She wrote that she had suspicions there's something bad in a foundation of one of the buildings on campus as well as a garden. She has to mean Tony's memorial garden."

"When were you going to tell me this?"

"Sorry, but when it was fresh in my mind, I was running for my life and wheezing half to death."

Gene's jaw tensed. He was driving more reasonably now. "The garden, a foundation, and Rosa isn't sick."

"Come to think of it," I said, "of all our classmates, you and I don't seem to have gotten off too badly."

"Yet," Gene added, eyebrow arched, "but we still haven't gotten off scot-free either."

I chewed my lip for a second, thinking. "Give me a list of who's sickest from our class."

"Gloria Benevento. Rocco Cargione. Heather Fucilla. Donna Illardo. Tony Nuccio."

"Stop there. Weren't they all jocks?"

Gene made a confused grimace. "They were all basketball players. Why?"

"They all spent a lot of time in the gym, the one that was built between fifth and sixth grade. Rosa, you and I never played CYO sports. The only time we were in the gym was for gym class and—"

"During our sixth grade service project, cleaning up all the construction dust once the gym was built."

"Then painting it. It was us and the public school kids who went to CCD."

"Turo's wife was one of those," Gene said. "I recognized her at the viewing."

I was startled. "How on earth do you remember things like that?"

"I never forget a face."

"I remember that Rosa wasn't there for any of those project days. I remember her telling everybody that she finished her confirmation service hours doing chores for her grandfather."

Gene frowned, thinking. "She didn't help build Tony's garden at all, did she?"

I replayed memories of that week, of sweating in the sun, of the smell of PABA sunscreen on my skin and Gene's, of the steamy stench of the grass withering under the hazy sun. I thought of all the faces there, but Rosa's did not show up. "Gene, whatever we're looking for isn't in your creek water samples anyway. It's buried in the gym foundation and planted in that garden."

Gene glanced at me quickly before returning his eyes to the road. "Whoever put it there thinks we already have evidence that they did. They think we know something we don't."

I laughed softly, bitterly. "They think we're smarter than we actually are."

Gene pulled into the driveway, behind a Walkerville Police van. His mom still lived in the same apartment after all these years. It was half of an old twin house, bricks and white trim, with a wooden porch full of container flowers that seemed to glow with color in the late spring twilight. The screen door was propped open, the storm door behind that open as well.

Just as Gene unbuckled and threw open his door, my phone rang. I checked the caller ID. "It's Dr. Heckler. I should take this. Go to your mom."

As my phone rang a second time, Gene scowled at me. "No. I'm not leaving you alone with Bobby right behind us."

"I just told you not ten minutes ago that I took a self-defense class."

"How long ago was that?" Gene slid back inside the car and slammed the door shut. He hit the automatic lock button. "I'm not leaving you."

Third ring. I rolled my eyes and answered the call. "Dr. Heckler?"

"Yes, hi, Cate. I have some results for you."

"Can I put you on speaker, Dr. Heckler? Gene—Dr. Marcasian is here. He probably wants to hear this too."

"By all means."

I hit the "speaker" button, and Dr. Heckler continued. "Like I said, I have results, but I can't say I have explanations."

Gene and I exchanged looks. "That's better than nothing," I said.

"I checked for dioxin, like you suggested, but nothing came up."

I nearly leapt out of my seat. Bobby was banging on my window. Shaking, I clung to my phone with one hand and held up a hand to Bobby.

"No other common environmental toxins came up either," Dr. Heckler said. "So Dr. Breen ran it through a more in-depth molecular analysis, and we found something. Dr. Marcasian, are you familiar with nitrosureas?"

The corners of Gene's eyes crinkled in concentration. "The DNA alkylating agents?"

"The very same," Dr. Heckler said. "We found nitrosureas in the form of BiCNU in every single sample you swabbed."

"BiCNU? Isn't that carmustine?"

"What's carmustine?" I asked Gene.

"It's a chemotherapy drug," Gene explained, his voice wondering. "My mom had it implanted in her brain after one of her tumors was removed."

Dr. Heckler continued, "We also found some other agents in the sample in smaller amounts. Since BiCNU needs to be refrigerated, I'm wondering if what you sampled might be a new compound, designed to give BiCNU shelf-stability."

"Dr. Heckler," I asked, "what does this bick-new feel like? I mean, if I were to touch it with my fingers?"

Bobby thumped more insistently on my window. "JUST A SECOND," I shouted. I turned from the window so I wouldn't have to look at him.

I could hear the dismay in Dr. Heckler's voice. "It would feel oily at room temperature, but I wouldn't recommend touching it with ungloved hands if you can help it. Carmustine is pretty potent. It passes the blood-brain barrier. It's infamous for messing with the lungs of the patients who take it. Pneumonia is a common side-effect."

Gene's eyes flew to mine. "Sister Thomas Marie died of pneumonia."

"MARY CATHERINE, TIME'S UP," Bobby shouted at my window.

"Thanks, Doctor Heckler. Gotta go." I hung up. Gene and I shared one more meaningful look before we jumped out of his car.

"Is everything all right?" I asked.

For all the banging on my window, Bobby completely ignored me. Chin lifted, he addressed Gene. "Don't you want to see if your mom is okay?"

Gene sped to my side, insinuating himself between Bobby and me. "Of course. Where is she?"

Bobby gestured for us to head into the apartment. Gene took me by the wrist and pulled me close to his side then led the way. We ascended the porch steps, and I smelled the lavender in the stone urn by the doorway, the moonflowers opening in the side yard. My heart was beating harder than Bobby had pounded on my window.

Gene pulled me through the little tiled foyer into the living room. The walls were different, the furniture simpler, but the layout was the same as it had been in 1987. There was the same crucifix over the entryway. The same picture of the Sacred Heart hung above their tiny fireplace. However, there was no evidence of any sort of break-in here. It was like, if I looked hard enough, I could have seen our preteen selves, Gene and me, books in hand, feet pulled guiltily off of the coffee table as Mrs. Marcasian brought us iced teas.

But there was no Mrs. Marcasian here now. Instead I saw Frank Farzza standing, hands on hips, chest inflated, in the middle of the Marcasians' living room.

I heard a dull clanking then a series of speedy clicks. I felt Gene's hand ripped away from me. By the time I turned to him, Bobby already had Gene's hands cuffed behind his back.

Gene said nothing about that. "Where's my mother, Campobello?"

"Hear that?" Frank mocked. "I haven't even touched him yet and he's crying for his momma."

Bobby shoved the handcuffed Gene towards a smirking Frank. "Mary Catherine, do you remember telling Gene in Pub Mo Thóin that he could 'finish this later?'"

I was shaking too hard to speak.

Bobby turned to Frank. "Finish it."

Bobby pinned my arms behind my back and brought me to my knees to make me watch. Frank threw Gene to the floor. I could not move as Frank aimed kick after kick at Gene's ribs and face. Then I felt a hard whack at the base of my skull, and I went out cold.

CHAPTER FIFTEEN
TRUE BLUE

"Cate? Catie?"

Why was Staz whispering like that?

"Catie, come on, wake up."

Why was Staz even here? And where was "here?"

I mumbled something like "What time is it?" I tried moving my head off of the cool, wet grass, but all that did was make me vomit. When I finished throwing up, I became acutely aware of the pain shooting through my neck and out my ears, eyes, temples, everywhere.

"Catie, they knocked me out. I think they used chloroform, whoever they are."

"Chloro—" I tried moving again. This time I didn't puke, but I did stir up more skull pain. I managed to open my eyes, but everything was dim. I could smell wet earth, warm trees, and I could taste the sting of my own sick on the tip of my tongue. "You were—?"

"Kidnapped. Seriously."

"Staz, where are we?"

"I have no clue."

I heard voices, three male voices, talking hurriedly in hushed tones somewhere behind us. My eyes adjusted to the moonlight and I could make out Staz's features right in front of me. She was curled up in fetal position, facing me. The hand lying on the ground was holding her belly. The other hand was braced against her lower back. She was wearing an outfit I knew to be her pajamas. The waistband of the light green sweatpants bottom was slung low, leaving plenty of room for her pregnant belly to protrude comfortably.

"Staz." My voice sounded warped and stupid, as if it were coming out of a paper towel tube. "Why are your pants wet?"

Staz is not a crier. When she started to shake and sob, I knew the answer.

I made it to my hands and knees. "When did contractions start?"

"I don't know. A while ago. I came to in a small place. It felt like a car trunk, but I was blindfolded. I got moved to a van, and there was already somebody else in there. A little while later, he threw two people in with us. They didn't take my blindfold off 'til we got here."

"Did you see who it was that took you?"

"No. Some bloody coward snuck up behind me in the driveway as I was heading out for a milkshake. He covered my face with something, and I passed out."

I lifted my head and was rewarded with a fresh wave of nausea, but within a few seconds I knew where we were. The smell of the algae, the sound of creek water splashing against rocks, and just a few hundred yards away the cement legs of the railroad bridge. We were in the deepest valley, the place where no one can hear you scream. This was Quaker Creek. This was where I had found the body of Tony Vitale.

"You said 'us.' Who else is here besides you, me and Gene?"

"Hi, Mary Catherine."

I recognized the voice immediately. "Mrs. Marcasian?"

She gave a little, dry laugh. "Sorry, dear. I was hoping we could catch up somewhere less outdoorsy."

Even here, she could find calm and joy. "Where's Gene?"

A dull, moaning, honking sound came from somewhere near Mrs. Marcasian's voice.

I squinted in the twilight and aimed my voice at Gene's mom. "How bad is he?"

"Pretty bad," said another voice, this one horrifyingly cheerful.

I looked up, and there was Frank Farzza again. Dizzied, I dropped my head.

"I believe in God," Mrs. Marcasian began, just above her breath, "the Father Almighty, Creator of heaven and earth..."

Frank dug his toe into my ribs. Against my will, I cried out at the pain.

"Get up," he said.

"Make me."

I heard a speedy series of clicks and felt the cold mouth of a handgun pressed against my throbbing temple. I felt one more wave of nausea—from fear or brain injury, I don't know—and turned my face to Frank's. For the first time in my life, I was glad that my behavior was being fueled by a raging case of PMS.

"Make me."

Frank's smile spread under his hawk nose. Staring me down, he took the gun from my head and aimed it at Staz's belly.

"Catie, no. Whatever he says, don't."

I got up.

"...and the life of the world to come, Amen." Mrs. Marcasian was praying the rosary. "Our Father, who art in heaven..."

Frank nodded at me. Suddenly Bobby was at his side. I felt myself sway on my feet. Instinctively, I put out my hands for balance, and Bobby caught me. I was too sick to recoil, but oh boy did I want to.

Bobby took my face in his hands. "Mary Catherine, I'm so, so sorry."

"Did you actually pistol-whip me?" It was the only thing I could think to ask.

"I am really, really sorry, but I had to."

Mrs. Marcasian prayed on, as if none of us were there. "Blessed are you among women..."

"You *had* to pistol-whip her?" Staz demanded, incredulous.

"Shut up, Jew," Frank snarled.

"No problem, Dago," she snapped back in spite of the tears still in her voice.

Frank moved to backhand her across the face, but Bobby caught his arm. "Farzza, no."

"Your last name is Fart-za? And you made fun of *Cate's* last name?"

Frank tugged to get his arm out of Bobby's grip, but Bobby was stronger. He twisted Frank's arm and threw him to the ground, making him land nearly where Gene's crumpled body lay. Then Bobby turned back to me.

He draped my arm over his shoulders and led me away a few yards. His voice became saccharine. "Can I get you an ice pack for your head?"

Um, how about letting us all go? "Bobby, what do you want from me? What do you want from Gene? His mom? Staz? Can't you see she's in labor?"

"You call her 'Staz'? That's cute. When you gave me her address, you said her name was Anastasia."

"Catie!" Staz shrieked. "Why did you give him my address?"

"He's a cop, Staz! He said he needed my emergency contact!"

Staz shook her head violently. "Forget it. Not your fault. His fault. Oh, by the way, I had an ultrasound yesterday. Baby's still breech. I'm gonna need more than a little help here."

No wonder my usually devil-may-care Staz was so deeply panicked. I waited for Gene to move, speak, do something, anything. He remained silent.

Mrs. Marcasian said, "...and at the hour of our death—"

"You'd better pray," Frank sneered at Gene's mom. "'Cause if they don't give us what we want, now *is* the hour of your death."

Mrs. Marcasian's voice stopped. She fixed her eyes on Frank, swallowed hard, then said, "Amen. Hail Mary, full of grace..."

The third man stepped forward. I could barely discern the details of his face in the dusky light, but what I could see made me step back. My addled brain thought it was seeing a ghost. He was the same height, if a little broader at the shoulder than his childhood self had been. He had traded his CYO basketball jersey for a suit and tie.

"Tony?" I whispered.

The finely creased face flinched. The blue eyes blinked. "No. Just Chris."

Chris Vitale, *capodecina* of Hantzel-Brace-Courton's Walkerville Branch. I backed away another step, but Bobby's arm braced me, keeping me in place. With his other hand he stroked my curls. Staz's eyes shut tightly, and she doubled over, a cry escaping from her tightened lips. Gene's mother, hands tied behind her back, jostled her son with her foot. Gene remained still. I found it quite difficult not to vomit again.

"Bobby wants what I want, Mary Catherine," Chris said in the same smooth, confident voice I imagined him using at board meetings. "He wants what everyone in Walkerville wants. Security. A thriving community."

"Maybe that's why I moved out of Walkerville," I said. "I would rather have the ugly truth, thanks very much."

Bobby turned to face me. His dark curls had tightened with all the humidity. His face was beaded with sweat, some of it rolling down through his stubble. "I can give you the truth, Mary Catherine. I love you."

"You're kidding me, right?" Staz laughed. "You bludgeon all the women you love?"

This time Bobby was not able to restrain Frank's hand. Staz lifted her face when Frank had retreated. I saw a dark trickle slipping down the side of her mouth. We locked eyes. I shook my head, trying to tell her, *Shut up, would you!*

Bobby didn't seem to hear any of this. "I love you. I've loved you for decades now. You were like nobody I ever met before. All you have to do is give Chris what he wants. Agree to stay quiet. Then I can take you away from all the trouble you're in. Nobody will bother you again."

I gave him my most confused look. "What trouble am I in? And how are Gene and I supposed to give Chris what he wants when he just said he wants security and thriving and economic blah-blah-blah?"

Yeah, I know. I'm a writer and should have had better command of the language, but I was nursing a pretty harsh knock to the brain.

Chris glanced at Frank then jerked his head toward where Gene lay. Frank yanked me from Bobby's arms and threw me down next to Gene. My head felt like it might roll off my shoulders if I got one more jolt. Somehow I managed to look at Gene long enough to see that, while his eyes might be closed and his nose might look like a balloon, at least he was still breathing.

Frank planted his feet right in front of us and looked down his nose. "Give us the stuff you took from Sister's office."

I swallowed bile and tried to think of a response. When I was too slow, Frank grabbed me by the shoulders of my new blouse and shook me. "I sai—"

"I heard what you said." I closed my eyes from the

pain. "I just don't know what you're looking for. I'm sure you checked my purse after Bobby knocked me out. You didn't find anything there, or you wouldn't be asking me now. What exactly do you want, Frank?"

"The evidence you took," Bobby explained, still keeping his voice as soft as he would use talking to a child. "Whatever you took from Sister's office, we need to keep it quiet. We can't have people knowing what happened at Seven Dolors. They'll close the school. They'll close HBC. You'll destroy the whole town. People were mean enough to you in grade school. You want things to be even worse than that?"

I felt Gene twitch behind me. I placed my hands behind my back as if I were bracing myself, but I felt as subtly as I could for Gene's hands.

"As it was in the beginning," Mrs. Marcasian whispered, "is now and ever shall be..."

My fingertips brushed Gene's. He lifted his fingers and placed them on top of mine. That was my security.

"We know you took something from Dolors," Frank stepped closer to us. "Tell us where it is, or we kill one of them."

I edged further back into Gene, far enough to feel the rise and fall of his chest against my lower back. I could have sworn that I felt Gene's fingers pushing mine in the direction of the top of his body. Hoping I understood him, that he was even communicating with me at all, I edged in that direction, giving Frank my most frightened face, hoping he would take my movement as done in terror of his power over our loved ones.

I looked over at Bobby. He took my attention on him as encouragement. "Mary Catherine, I got your fingerprints from the bag that's holding Turo's note. I was able to transfer your prints onto the gun he used."

Staz snorted. "Is that even possible?"

"He's a cop," Frank said over his shoulder. "He knows what he's doing."

"Possible or not," Bobby said, "it doesn't look good for you. I was really close to getting a warrant for your arrest, especially since Turo was shot with your gun."

"She's only barely owned a gun," Staz countered, "and that was, like, sixteen years ago."

Bobby shook his head at me in a pitying fashion. "That's not what the records show. Not anymore, anyway. Think, Mary Catherine. If I can make it appear that you've owned a gun all this time, I can make both of us disappear—just like Rosa did with her family. We can travel the world, totally free. Just give Chris the samples he needs, and I'll take you away. I can treat you the way I should have treated you all those years ago—the way you deserve to be treated. I can make up for letting you be the one to find Tony when it was really me who found him first."

"It was really Bobby who killed my brother," Chris said, his voice as cold and even as the edge of a knife. "Bobby wasn't the one who put cyanide in the amaretti cookies. His dad did, just following orders. But Bobby was the good boy who followed orders and fed them to Tony."

"Your dad shouldn't have called the EPA in the first place," Frank said to Chris. "The family was finally doing good, with all the contracts from HBC, then your dad had to go and try to bring in the feds."

Chris shrugged as if it didn't matter. "He was worried once he found out Tony had been poisoned with the gym cleanup project. But Tony's death was a message. My father got the message. He shut up. He towed the line. He taught me to be a better player than he ever was."

I watched Bobby curl into himself like a slug being

doused with salt. He shook silently for a moment before I heard him draw in a sobbing breath. So what Chris was saying, with no grief at all for his little lost brother, could only be true.

"Listen," Chris said to me. "My father wouldn't let it go, and it lost me my little brother. Sister Thomas Marie wouldn't let it go, and look what happened to her."

Mrs. Marcasian was still praying. "Oh my Jesus, forgive us our sins. Save us from the fires of hell..."

"Carmustine on the keyboard instead of poison cookies?" I guessed.

Chris just shrugged again, a gesture that seemed so practiced I wondered if he had any soul left at all. "Not pure carmustine. One of our experimental compounds. And now that you know how Turo killed Sister, you're going to have to tell us where you sent that evidence, or Frank here will have to—"

"If Turo killed Sister, why kill him and pin it on me?"

Chris walked over to Bobby and pulled him back up to a standing position. Bobby dragged the back of his hand across his eyes. Chris made his way back to me.

"You don't want us to find the people who did your work for you?"

I eyed Frank's gun. "Can't say that I do."

"We don't want our people found out either. But this is why bullies always win, see. You care about the people close to you. We only care about ourselves. That's why we can kill these two and not blink an eye if you won't give us what you took."

"And keep quiet about it," Frank added helpfully.

I looked at Staz. Gritting her teeth, she shook her head.

I looked at Mrs. Marcasian. Her face had a calm I wish I could have summoned. Then I might know how to get us out of this situation.

She said, "...especially those in most need of thy mercy."

Then I saw her look at Gene, crumpled behind me. She bowed her head, unable to bless herself for the restraints on her hands. She teetered to one side, tottered to another, then she stood up and faced Chris Vitale.

"Mary Catherine has nothing to give you," Gail Marcasian said. "Why don't you start by killing me?"

"Okay," said Frank, and he put a bullet through the back of her head.

I screamed so loudly that I did not hear the report of the shot that felled Frank less than a second later.

CHAPTER SIXTEEN
THE WARRIOR

Another shot fired. Two more. I saw Chris draw his own handgun with a flash of flat gray, then he ducked for cover behind a nearby tree. Bobby threw himself over me, which in turn landed me on top of Gene. I heard Gene cry out in response. That was the best sound I'd heard for an hour or so. It meant he was still alive.

My terror was starting to turn to anger. "Bobby, if you really love me, you'll get off me and help my pregnant friend over there. You know, the one you kidnapped?"

"I didn't kidnap her. It was Frank."

"Oh, that makes *everything* better. Go help her."

Bobby shook his head so vehemently that his sweat-damp curls danced on his head. "I'm not leaving you."

I kneed him in the groin and rolled him off. As Bobby clutched and moaned, I army-crawled along the dewy creek bank until I reached Mrs. Marcasian.

I heard Gene groan and saw him twist to stand up, but he collapsed back to the ground with a cry. I could not see Frank, but I could hear sickening sucking, gurgling sounds coming from his chest.

I placed my head just under Gene's mom's chin. Her neck was slick with blood. I followed the trail of blood up to the side of her head. The complete lack of anything but blood and softness was so alarming to me that I yanked my hand back and pressed it to my already filthy shirt. Just then, though, I noticed her chest moving slightly, like the fluttering of a moth's wing.

Then I noticed that the gunfire had stopped.

I looked up the slope above the creek, the direction from which the non-Frank shots had been fired. Two people stood up there, barely silhouetted by the half-moon. One was average height with a cloud of hair around her face. The other was a stooped figure shuffling its way down toward us.

"Now, *bambina*?" a familiar voice said. "Now can we call the cops?"

"*Nonno*, please. I'll take care of this."

That voice I could place, but I could not believe my ears. I called out, "Rosa?"

She did not answer, but the first voice replied, "*Catarina, bella*! Are you all right? Did this stinking, church-burning *cafone* put his hands on you?"

"Mr. Celli?" I squeaked.

"Which stinking, church-burning *cafone* did you mean?" Staz yelled. "The one you just shot, the cop-gone-bad, or the coward hiding behind the tree?"

Rosa took her grandfather's arm and helped him down the slope to us. "Who's hiding behind a tree?"

"Chris Vitale." I said, amazed at how calm my voice sounded considering I'd just put my hand into a gunshot wound. "He's got a gun."

Rosa seemed surprised by neither the appearance of Tony's big brother nor by the fact that he was armed and cowering nearby. She lifted her own gun again. "Which tree?"

"*Bambina*, the police, now."

"I don't think he's talking about you," Staz mock-whispered at Bobby, who was still curled around himself.

Rosa was now standing a few feet from me and Mrs. Marcasian. She looked down at the two of us, pointed the barrel of her gun at the ground, and handed it back to Mr. Celli.

"Here." She handed me the cardigan she was wearing. "For her head."

I took it and placed it gingerly over the wound. The Girl Scout in me wanted to apply direct pressure, but I did not want to squeeze what brain the bullet had left her. The complete uselessness of my gesture tapped a crack in my shock. A sob formed in my tightened throat. I spoke around it.

"Gene. Wake up. We need a doctor."

"Help me," he said.

I swallowed the sob and dove for his hand. "What can I do? Your mom—"

"I know."

"And my friend Staz is in labor."

"I know."

"I have a crappy bandage on your mom's head. She's still breathing."

Gene winced, coughed, then winced harder. "How much?"

I hesitated. "Breathing? Not much."

"Leave my mom. Help me over to your friend."

"Gene, your mother was *shot* in the *head*."

Gene looked at me through puffy lids. He trembled just with the effort of breathing. "My mother took a bullet for a pregnant woman. She wants me to save that baby."

I heard a sound that scared me even more than the sound of the gunfire: a rarely-frightened Staz crying again.

Mr. Celli scooted over to Staz and dropped to his knees by her side. "Does anybody have a phone?"

"I think that church-burning *cafone* has mine," Staz answered.

"Would you all just shut up and let me take care of things?" Rosa took her gun back from Mr. Celli—her grandfather, I now realized—and she pulled her phone out of her left pocket. She thumbed at it for a second, then she was on the phone with 911.

"Yes, Quaker Creek, down by the railroad bridge. One gunshot wound to the head, one woman in labor. My name? Trini Ross. No, no relation."

Another shot flew out from behind Chris Vitale's tree. It just hit the leaf mulch at Rosa's feet.

"You're a lousy shot, you know?" Rosa ended her call and put her phone back into her pocket. "The rest of you, stay down. He's after me now, not you."

"You sure about that, Trinaglia?" Chris yelled back.

"Keep talking, *chiacchierone*," Mr. Celli gestured with his left hand, the one not holding the gun. "That way the cops can hear where you're hiding."

"Mary Catherine." Gene's voice sounded weaker. "Get me to your friend."

I could think of a million reasons to say no, but I could think of a million and one to say yes. I slid my arm under his earthbound shoulder and tried helping him up, but his hands were still bound. He cried out and fell back to the ground.

I looked over and saw Rosa watching us. I asked, "A little help?"

Rosa trained her gun away from the tree line and down at Bobby Campobello. "Bobby, give me the keys to Gene's cuffs, before another girl gets you in the *stugots*. While you're at it, hand over your gun. Safety on, please."

He stopped writhing long enough to throw a key ring at her, then he lay his gun in the dirt. She kept her gun on him as she squatted down to pick them up. He looked over at me, and I saw that he had a bloody nose. I hadn't hit him in the nose, had I?

Rosa handed Bobby's gun to me.

"I don't want it."

"I do," Gene said.

Staz yelled through another contraction. I followed the

sound with my eyes and saw that Mr. Celli had put his gun down and was holding both of Staz's hands.

Rosa had now made it over to Gene and me. As Rosa set him free, Gene shouted, "Tell her to get on her hands and knees."

Staz groaned. "You want me to do *what* now?"

Gene gritted his teeth then said, "Mr. Celli, help her move. It will help with the pain, and it will help make more room for the baby if we need to deliver here."

"We?" I demanded.

"We are way deep in the forest," Rosa said. "It's going to be a while before anyone gets here. We are all we have."

Gene nodded. "I have several cracked ribs and probably a concussion. I can barely breathe. I can barely move my arms. I can talk you through this, but I need your help."

I spoke into his blood-crusted ear. "Gene, we don't have towels, hot water or string, and an MBA is shooting at us from the woods."

Gene closed his eyes and tilted his head, as if preparing to talk to a simpleton. "Then you're going to have to work extra hard."

"Catie? It hurts. I'm scared."

Staz's fear sent a lightning bolt of awareness through my shock. The adrenaline that had been coursing through my veins seemed to bottom out. My brain was telling my body: *If Staz is afraid, then we are doomed. RUN AWAY!*

I bit my lip, hard, just so I could feel something, *anything* but terror. Then I forced myself to laugh. "What are you talking about? If anyone can give sass in the face of danger, it's gotta be you."

She shook her head. Her voice was raw as she said, "I can't. Not anymore."

My voice cracked as I said, "You just have to keep it up until help gets here, and that should be soon. Right, Rosa?"

Rosa met my eyes through the darkness. I saw her hesitate. Then she nodded. "Soon."

Gene turned to Rosa. "Can you cover us? And help my mom?"

Rosa did not even stop to nod. She pointed her barrel down at the ground and sidled over to Mrs. Marcasian. Then she began yelling into the trees about how Chris should just give up now that the cops were on their way. Chris answered with another couple of shots that hit nothing.

Rosa cackled. "I guess they don't teach aim in business school?"

Mr. Celli was congratulating Staz for rolling over onto her hands and knees. "Doctor, does this look good?"

I could not read his expression for all the swelling around his nose, but his voice sounded resigned. "It looks as good as its going to get."

"It's not gonna get any better, I can tell you that." From that crack, I could tell Staz was between contractions.

"What kind of breech is the baby?" Gene asked.

"Frank breech."

Gene closed his eyes and nodded. "That's what I was hoping you'd say. This is not impossible, but it's not going to be easy. Are you comfortable having Mary Catherine check to see if the baby's emerging yet?"

I turned and gaped at Gene. "You mean—?"

Staz laughed. "He means you and I are about to bring our friendship to a whole new level."

I was too relieved to be grossed out. "See? Danger-shmanger. There's that Staz-sass we all know and love."

Mr. Celli leaned into the conversation. "What can I do?"

Gene swallowed hard. "Go check on Bobby and Frank, then tell me their injuries."

Mr. Celli looked like he was about to argue. Then he just crawled on hands and knees back to our fallen classmates, muttering, "*Madonna mia*," all the way.

"How are you doing—" Gene whispered to me, "What's her name again?"

"Staz."

"How are you feeling, Staz?"

"Other than fearing for my life and my nearly born kid's? Peachy."

"Did getting into this position help at all?"

Her answer was grudging but honest. "Yeah. It took the pressure off my back. Thanks for that."

"Don't thank me," Gene again closed his eyes briefly in relief. "Thank physics."

I couldn't help but snicker. "Hey, Staz, still think physics is for—?"

"Rosa, how's my mom?"

"She's lost a lot of blood, but she's still breathing."

With supreme effort, Gene filled his lungs. "Mom? Can you hear me?"

Nothing. Rosa confirmed, "She didn't even flinch, Gene."

Gene pressed his lips together then choked back a sob.

"Gene, I'm sorry," I said.

He shook his head and gritted his teeth again. "There's still life. There's still hope. Mr. Celli?"

"The Farzza boy, he's bleeding bad, not breathing so much. The Campobello boy? He's got a bloody nose and isn't moving."

Gene and I exchanged looks. I asked, "Is he breathing?"

"*Si, si*," said Mr. Celli. "Did you punch him in the nose, *Catarina*?"

"No. Think lower. A lot lower."

Mr. Celli jerked his head in assent. "He deserved it, *cafone*. Not as much as that Vitale boy, though. I don't care if his little brother was killed by the family. That's no excuse for trying to stop a nun by setting her church on fire."

Again I looked to Gene, but he seemed just as confused as I. "What are you talking about, Mr. Celli?"

Rosa did not look up from Mrs. Marcasian. "He's talking about how Sister Thomas asked Chris Vitale to help discover and clean up any toxic waste that might be hidden on campus."

In the stillness that followed, I listened for any rustling that might indicate Chris was still nearby, still listening to this further damning of his character. I heard nothing but the continued gurgling of life from Frank Farzza's lungs.

"Tell them, *bambina*. Tell them how he got the Farzza boy to leave Sister a threatening note, then tell her how he rewired the sacristy so bad it caught fire like it was all an accident."

"*Nonno*, I think you just did."

"Spaghetti," Bobby said.

I swung my head around to glare at Bobby. "What the —?"

"Spaghetti caught fire. G. I. Joe."

I looked back at Bobby and his eyes seemed just as clear as ever, but he looked as confused by his words as we were.

"What does that mean, 'spaghetti caught fire'?" I demanded.

"And why bring poor, innocent G. I. Joe into it?" Staz added.

Bobby shook his head. "I—I don't know."

Rosa looked up from Mrs. Marcasian and stared at

Bobby wonderingly. "Bobby. Are you sick?"

Before he could answer, Staz screamed, a visceral, deep howl that I felt rip through her back, where I'd rested my hand. "I think I'm supposed to be telling you to breathe," I said.

"*You* breathe, then!" This was followed by a string of curses in Yiddish and English. "I want Geoff here!"

Gene dragged himself closer. "Mary Catherine, can you lift my arm for me? Staz, is it all right if I try to examine you?"

"Oh, thank you," I said, though to Gene or God, I'm not sure.

"I don't care anymore," she sobbed. "Just get him out!"

"It's a boy?" I shrieked. "How did you keep it from me?"

"I found out yesterday at the ultrasound. Couldn't wait anymore."

"Mary Catherine," Gene said, "take my hand."

He held out a bruised arm, and my concussion and I helped him closer to Staz. He cried out once, twice, then was on his knees. He pulled in one breath, two, then looked at me. "I think I'll be okay. You go check on Mr. Celli."

I gulped then nodded. "Staz, I'm just stepping over to check on the hurt people. Gene will take great care of you."

"Come back, Catie!"

"I will." I scuttled over to Mr. Celli and the other two victims, still listening for any sign of Chris. Nothing. I looked at Rosa, asking her with my eyes for a sign that Mrs. Marcasian was okay. Now both Rosa and Mrs. Marcasian were covered in blood. I shuddered.

"Ow! That hurts!" Another stream of curses.

"Sorry," Gene said. "I just need to check the position of the baby."

"And?" I shouted over my shoulder.

"Not long," Gene said so breathlessly I could barely hear.

"Doctor?" Mr. Celli said. His voice had a calm that reminded me of Mrs. Marcasian praying. "The Farzza boy, he's not doing too good."

"Mary Catherine," Gene said, "switch."

I did not stop to think, intoxicated on a cocktail of both adrenaline and shock. We both struggled to our feet, both struggled to dash past each other. As we did, another shot flew out at us from the direction of the trees lining the creek. The shot missed us both. I dove for Staz and grabbed her under the shoulders, dragging her behind the nearest tree.

"What are you doing?"

"Finding cover. Didn't that midwife tell you that moving around helps labor progress?"

"Shut up and help me re-assume the position."

I looked across the now smoky clearing at Rosa, her grandfather, Gene, and all three patients. Gene was checking Frank's pulse, ripping open Frank's polo shirt and examining the wound itself. To my disbelief, Gene cursed.

"It's in the lung. I can't even do CPR on him."

"I had to stop him." Rosa, now cradling Mrs. Marcasian's head in her elbow, sounded not at all apologetic.

Gene tried a deep breath and shouted again, almost as loudly as Staz just had. "VITALE! ENOUGH! FARZZA'S—!"

Gene collapsed with the effort of pushing his cracked ribs. In the stillness that followed, I heard the distant sound of a weapon being reloaded.

"Gene," I called, "Staz needs you."

Gene lifted his head. He looked like he was about to give up.

"Doctor," Mr. Celli said in a low voice, "you are a good boy. You did all you can. Go save the momma. Go save that baby."

Gene shook his head, as if he either couldn't make sense of Mr. Celli's words or just couldn't bring himself to do any of it. Then he looked in the direction of his mother's body, the blood still flooding out of her. He made a sound as if he were being pierced with a hundred knives, then he heaved himself to his feet and hurled himself back in our direction.

As I rose to my knees and caught him mid-fall, I heard Mr. Celli praying over Frank's slowing breaths. *"Ave Maria, piena di grazia..."*

"Is he changing colors?" Bobby asked. I caught his expression that followed: confused, frustrated.

"He doesn't know what he's saying." Rosa's voice sounded as steady as her grandfather's now. "Gene, your mom is still breathing. EMTs should be here soon. She'll be okay."

"She'll be okay no matter what," Gene said just under his breath.

"E benedetto è il frutto del tuo seno, Gesú."

"Get ready," Gene said in my ear. "When she pushes the baby out, I'm going to need you to help get the baby up to her arms."

"Santa Maria, Madre di Dio."

"Can I push yet?"

"Just one more minute," he replied. "It won't be long. I want you as dilated as possible, to help the baby through. You'll have to hang in there."

Staz howled. I had to ask. "Is that from having to wait, or from another contraction?"

"BOTH!"

"*Prega per noi pecca—*" Mr. Celli paused. "Doctor, he's stopped breathing!"

"Does he have a pulse?"

"Wait, wait...yes, he does. *Cafone* is hanging in there too, just like Catarina's friend. Ah, there's another breath."

"Then keep praying," Gene said. "Staz, one more minute."

"*Prega per noi peccatori.*"

"There, was that a minute?"

Gene almost smiled. "Not quite."

"You're doing great, sweetness."

Staz didn't even answer me. She was just panting like something from a Bill Cosby routine.

I leaned into Gene's ear. "How soon will help get here?"

"Not soon enough," he admitted in a whisper. "Okay, Staz, it's time. One big push."

I was not prepared for the grossness that followed. I'm not sure I'm up for describing it all. I remember Gene expressing relief that there wasn't much blood, so that made me feel better. I don't think I heard anything in those moments but Gene telling Staz to push, Staz's guttural cries as she obeyed someone for the first time in her life, and then, just before that final push—

"*Adesso e nell'ora della nostra morte.*"

—then that first cry—

"Doctor," Mr. Celli called out, "he's gone."

—Staz's laughing, sobbing relief. Gene's pushing the baby into my arms, the slimiest lizard alien I had ever seen, and I loved him with a fury I didn't know I could have for a child not even my own.

"Staz, he's amazing." I brought him to his mother at last. She was a mass of sounds but no words.

Gene fell back with bloody hands and a shout of pain.

"Doctor? Did you hear? He's—"

"I heard," Gene said. "Amen."

"Amen," Mr. Celli echoed. He was silent for a moment. Then, after a series of grunts, he was on his feet and shouting at the creek. "Vitale! Your friend is dead! Your baby brother is dead! The good and the bad? It doesn't matter. They all die. There is nowhere you can hide from God, *bambino*. Your family, your company, they both make widows and orphans. What do you get from this, eh? What can you—?"

Like a ghost in a gray suit, Chris Vitale stepped out from behind a tree, just a few yards before me, just a few yards away from where I'd found his little brother's poisoned body. Then Chris leveled his gun at Mr. Celli.

"*NONNO!*" Rosa dropped Gene's mom and leapt to her feet.

Chris fired. Rosa caught her grandfather just as he fell with a bullet in his own chest.

Rosa let fly a stream of curses I could no longer define. A spray of blood spouted from Mr. Celli's lips. I could already tell he was bleeding much faster than Frank had. I looked up. Chris was gone. I followed Rosa's path with my eyes, and she stopped where Chris had just stood. I looked where she was looking, and there was a gray suit, writhing, writhing, and then so suddenly still.

Now Rosa was looking in Gene's direction, her face a white sheet of horrible awe. I followed her gaze again. I found Gene, slung on his side against the ground, Bobby's gun still smoking in his hand. Chris Vitale lay on the ground, letting fly his own stream of curses, lifting his hand from the wound in his shoulder, staring in fury at his blood dripping from his own fingers.

And that's when I finally heard the sirens, could see the

lights arriving, flashing red and blue over the slope, could see the silhouettes of our rescue. I crawled over to Mr. Celli. Out of the corner of my eye, I saw Rosa back away from Vitale's body and return to her grandfather. She fell to her knees next to me, and we each took one of his hands.

"*Ora lascia,*" Mr. Celli gurgled, "*o Signore, che il tuo servo vada...*"

"*In pace.*"   Rosa placed her fingers over her grandfather's eyes and closed them.

In pah-chay, I mouthed to myself. In peace. And now, Lord, let your servant go in peace.

In the chaos of state troopers and SWAT and paramedics and stretchers that followed, I clung to Mr. Celli's hand. Before long I was pried from him, dragged onto a stretcher of my own and assaulted with penlights in my eyes. In the stretcher next to mine, being lugged up the hill to the ambulances, was not Gene or Staz. It was Bobby.

"Chris," he said. "He lost a lot of gravy."

I closed my eyes. "You're probably right."

I got off easy. It took an x-ray, a CAT scan, an MRI, and an EEG to determine that all I had was a brutal concussion. I had to stay overnight for observation. I could have asked Staz and Geoff to observe me at home, but they were just a bit busy up on the maternity ward with their newborn. I was given a gown and a bed. All of my clothes were taken for evidence.

"I just got that top, too," I half-mourned to the collecting investigator.

The ER doctors warned me that nurses would be making me wake up every hour to be sure I wasn't having a brain bleed. That made me think of Frances Marcasian and how she had died. But even when I was not being given a series of field sobriety tests, I was being questioned by state police, then FBI, then state police again, then FBI again. At least my stream of guests garnered me a private room.

I asked about Gene. Confidentiality rules being what they were, they could not tell me his injuries or prognosis. I asked about Mrs. Marcasian and got the same response. That told me that she was probably still alive, otherwise what confidentiality would she have to protect? They told me that Chris Vitale was being treated at another hospital and would be moved to jail to await trial as soon as he was well enough.

"Is Bobby Campobello at the same hospital?" I asked the last FBI agent to visit.

He opened his mouth to give me the "confidentiality" bit, but then he stopped. "You said you noticed that his speech seemed unusual at times."

"More like nonsensical."

The agent nodded and made a grimace, as if to say, "I shouldn't be telling you this, but..."

"Bobby Campobello has been moved into the oncology ward."

"Cancer?" My voice came out pitifully high and weak. I remembered Rosa staring down at him, doubtful wonder on her face. *Bobby. Are you sick?* Then I thought of the battles Gene's mom had been fighting over the years. "Does he have a brain tumor?"

Again that "I shouldn't be telling you this" look. "I'm sorry. I can't tell you that he has tumors affecting his speech and motor functions."

I studied the agent's meaningful look that followed, then I nodded. It explained a lot: his non sequiturs, his inability to stand back up again after I'd kneed him, the spontaneous nosebleed. "Has anyone figured out why he tried to frame me for Turo DiFrancesco's suicide?"

"It wasn't a suicide, and we know it wasn't you."

I was relieved, horrified and confused. "How?"

"We found a copy of Turo's note on the network backup tapes for the Walkerville police station."

Could Bobby really have been that stupid? When in my shock I did not reply, the FBI agent explained, "From what we've been able to piece together from evidence, DiFrancesco was the one poisoning the principal. Farzza was keeping tabs on her electronic communications. Farzza found out that Sister was on to the likelihood that someone was after her, that she even suspected DiFrancesco. Campobello was seen going down to the church basement shortly before DiFrancesco was killed. It's really looking like—"

"Bobby did it. Then he wanted to make it look like I'd done it so I'd be scared enough to run away with him or something." I thought of the picture of Bobby's wife and daughter. I could tell that he loved them, didn't he? So why try to involve me in all of this? "He asked me to dance, at our eighth grade graduation. That's all."

The agent made a little conciliatory sound through his nose. "Sometimes brain tumors make people move, talk, and act in unusual ways."

I couldn't help but snicker. "So he's not actually obsessed with me. He's just dying."

"Do you know the whereabouts of Rosa Trinaglia, A. K. A. Trini Ross?"

I felt something throb in the back of my very sore neck because my jaw dropped so quickly—both at the rapid change of subject and the fact that the FBI even needed me to fill this in. "I was going to ask you the same question."

Apparently Rosa had disappeared so well that even her family's old contacts in the Witness Protection Program did not know where she'd gone. Did I have any idea?

Trini Ross, known for her literary fiction set in the Tuscan countryside? They'd probably figure it out on their own soon enough. "I wish I did."

A few hours later, I woke from a doze to find a nurse I hadn't met yet, smiling by my bed. She was pushing a wheelchair. "Good morning."

In spite of the officers keeping watch outside my room, I still gave her ID lanyard more than passing consideration. "Are you the new shift?"

She shook her head. "Nope. I'm Terry. I'm from the maternity ward. I was asked to come get you. No! Don't jump up. You'll give yourself a bleed."

I had to sign in on a clipboard at the double doors leading into the secure maternity unit. Then Terry knocked on the door to one of the rooms. Just hearing Geoff's voice saying, "Come in," was enough to get me crying. Within seconds Geoff was practically picking me up off my chair, his gangly arms wrapping all the way around me.

"Thank you, Cate." He dropped me long enough to rub his eye with the back of his hand. "They'd both be dead if it wasn't for you."

"Weren't," I corrected. "And she wouldn't have been in any danger to begin with if I hadn't given Bobby your address."

"And maybe," Staz shrilled, "if my husband had been home with me instead of off awarding plastic trophies to little kids in white pajamas, none of this would have happened at all."

Geoff rolled his eyes. "Well, if you hadn't convinced her to go to that funeral in the first place—"

I had to laugh. "Okay, enough! Let me see my fellow survivors."

Geoff stepped aside so I could be wheeled in the rest of the way. There was Staz, her hair sticking straight up in places, her contacts switched out for a retro-retro pair of John Lennon glasses. The baby boy was in her arms. Nurse Terry helped me up to kiss both of them on their adorable little foreheads. The baby's black hair was straight, like Geoff's, but stuck out in all directions, like Staz's. Already he had Geoff's thick eyebrows.

"How's he doing?"

Staz lifted her shoulders, and her face brightened with relief. "He's great. Turns out it's a good thing I did go early. I would've birthed an elephant if I'd waited another week."

I brushed his downy cheek with my knuckle. "Does he have a name yet?"

Staz and Geoff exchanged glances. Then they both looked to Terry. Terry nodded and headed for the door. "Let me just double check with the attending. If she okays it, I'll make a few calls, then I'll be back with another chair."

***

I don't know how all the gifts arrived so quickly. Already Mrs. Marcasian's ICU room was nearly transformed with construction paper cards, rainbow crayon "GET WELL MRS. MARKASEN" banners, and, while not one-thousand of them, there was a large number of paper cranes lined up along the windowsill just behind the ventilation screen.

Gene pointed to one taped to the wall just behind his mother's head. "This one's my favorite."

DEER MISSASS MARNANANAN,

MOMMY SAID YOU GOT HURT. PLEASE STOP GETTING SICK. I LOVE STORY TIME. I LOVE YOU.

YOUR BEST FRIEND,

GIANNA

P. S. I HOPE YOU DUNT DIE.

"I don't know whether to laugh or cry," I whispered.

Gene's eyes were red on the inside, black and blue on the outside. "Father Blaise was here already."

"Sacrament of the Sick?" I asked.

Gene nodded, keeping his eyes on his mom. I could barely see her face, she was so wound with bandages and white tape. Her free eye was held shut with a clear piece of tape. I don't know why that detail brought home the finality of her situation. Last night already seemed like it had happened to someone else somewhere else. Now, seeing the effects on someone I'd known since kindergarten breathed fresh life into that nightmare.

I had to get back to the present. "Gene?"

Gene blinked at me.

I turned and nodded at the figures who had accompanied me. They lurked just in the doorway, keeping a sacred distance between themselves and the *Pietà* of Gene and his dying mother.

I gestured to them. "Gene, you know Staz and her baby."

"Um, yeah, I think we've met," Staz said as Geoff pushed her a bit closer.

I introduced Geoff. Gene shook Geoff's hand but the action did not seem to register on his face.

"Thank you for saving them," Geoff said.

Gene shut his eyes and gave the slightest of nods.

"And thanks for changing my mind about physics," Staz added.

As he opened his eyes and gave Staz a quizzical expression, I reached for his hand. "How is your mom doing?"

He did not pull away. His voice was hoarse with exhaustion. "Now that the FBI and state troopers have their answers from me and their evidence from mom, I have to make a decision."

Before any of us could express shock or sympathy, Gene turned his eyes on the baby. His bruised, bandaged, tear-streaked face became radiant. "He looks great. Congratulations to you both."

"Thanks, man," Geoff said through a clenched throat. For perhaps the first time in her life, Staz was speechless.

Gene gave the baby another look, and his face wrinkled up in confusion. "Staz, how far along were you?"

"Thirty-five weeks. He's big for that, isn't he?"

"What was his birth weight? I mean, when they recorded it here, obviously."

"Eight pounds, two ounces." The pride in Geoff's voice was on the verge of being obnoxious.

"Was your estimated delivery based on date of last menstrual period or date of conception?"

Geoff shifted uncomfortably, and Staz shouted a quick, disbelieving laugh. "You're right, Cate. He's always on the clock."

Gene did not appear offended by this at all. "I'm asking because women who chart their cycles usually can pinpoint a date of conception, which makes determining the estimated date of delivery much more accurate than dating from last menstrual—"

"Gene?" I placed my other hand on his arm. "Take the day off. Be a son, not a doctor."

For the first time since last night, his fingers really responded to mine. He squeezed back, hard, and dropped his battered head into his free hand. Against medical advice, I rose from my wheelchair and placed my arm around his shoulder, resting my cheek against the top of his shuddering head.

"Dr. Marcasian?" A voice I did not know spoke at the door. It was the attending physician.

"Yes." Gene released my hand.

I backed away from him but did not return to my chair. "Do you want me to stay?"

He hesitated. He opened his mouth slightly, just enough to say, "No." Then he pressed his lips together, grimaced with the finality of the decision he was about to make. He nodded.

Geoff wheeled Staz and their son out to wait in the hallway. Two nurses took their place in the room. Even with my wheelchair and all the IV poles and ventilator cart, the room did not feel crowded. Maybe that's because to me the room was empty except for Gene and his mom.

The nurses told us they would be turning off the ventilator, as Gene requested. If she continued to breathe on her own, she would still receive pain medication, fluids and nutrition. If she stopped breathing, though, that was that.

"Wait," I said as a nurse put her hands to the ventilator. "I know they say that she can hear me even if she can't respond. Is that true?"

With practiced gentleness, she nodded. Her golden ponytail bounced, echoing a memory of Frances. "It's possible."

I nodded. I swallowed as much of the lump in my throat as I could. "Mrs. Marcasian? Thanks for—for all the popcorn. I'm sorry that I didn't keep in touch. I'm sorry that you had to die for me. Thank you for praying for me last night, even though I don't—"

I had to stop and take my hand from Gene's, press my fingers to my mouth. I had to get control back. I had to tell her. My head hurt, and my throat hurt, and something deep, deep in my belly hurt with this, but I had to let her know now, on this side of life. Because what if I were so far gone, what if I were so fallen away that she couldn't even hear me when she surely got to heaven?

"Even though I don't deserve it," I managed. "Thank you. Just, thank you."

"Mom." Gene took as deep a breath as his ribs would allow. "You were so loved, by everyone, even by Walkerville. The place killed you, but you loved them anyway. You were never one of them, and yet they treated you like family. How did you get them to do that?"

I thought of the Sacred Heart picture over the mantle in her living room. "She did it by being Jesus to others," I said just as I was realizing it for myself.

Gene was wracked with silent sobs that could only have caused his cracked ribs even more pain. He took my hand back in his and pulled me closer. I lowered my face against his shoulder as gently as I could. I did not want to hurt him any more.

Gene's other hand moved to mine, pressed something into my palm. I did not need to turn my face from his shoulder to know what it was that I now held. Beads that flowed from a crucifix.

"I can't," he rasped. "I want to. I just can't."

I heard the ventilator cart move, heard the squeak of nurses' sneakers on the polished tile floors. I heard the sucking and hissing of the ventilator, still going, still going.

I fumbled for the rosary. I wasn't even sure I would remember all the words, but for Gene, for his mom, I was willing to try.

I remembered Sister Thomas Marie starting the rosary at every May procession. I used her words. "Let us begin as we begin all good things, in the name of the Father, and of the Son, and of the Holy Spirit, Amen. I believe in God, the Father Almighty..."

Which mysteries to pray: the Sorrowful, to honor all this pain? But I always mixed up Scourging with the Crowning. The Joyful? They focused on the mother-son relationship that Jesus had with Mary. It sounded right, but it didn't feel right. And I didn't even know the new ones from John Paul II. After the first "Glory Be," I made up my mind.

"The first Glorious Mystery is the Resurrection. Our Father..."

Gail Marcasian took her last breath at the end of the fourth mystery, The Assumption of Mary into Heaven.

The nurse called the time of death. She touched Gene's shoulder, and then she left the room.

"It is finished," Gene said.

In the hall just beyond the door I heard fabric rip. I did not need to look to know that Staz must have torn a piece of her hospital gown, a Jewish sign of mourning.

***

As we had two concussions and a sorely stretched pelvis between the three of us, more transport was summoned to push Staz, Gene and me back to our respective rooms while Mrs. Marcasian's body was cared for.

"Gene," Geoff said as we waited for transport. "Staz and I would like to do something, if you don't object."

"Object?" he echoed, as if the syllables did not make sense to him.

Not surprisingly, Staz took over. "It's Jewish tradition to name a child after someone who has died. It's a—"

"—a way of keeping the memory of that person alive," Gene finished. "I may be Catholic, but I have plenty of Jewish friends from med school."

"Oh. Right." Staz was now flustered at not being as on top of the situation as she was used to being. "Anyway..."

Seeing Staz was not regaining her grip on the conversation, Geoff said, "We'd like to name our son Nicolo Gail."

Gene startled back in his chair, blinking fiercely.

Staz smiled through her own tears. "Nicolo, we found out, was Catie's neighbor's first name, Mr. Celli. Gail was your mom's name. Both of them gave their lives for all of us. It's the least—"

If she had even tried finishing her sentence, none of us would have heard it. We were all too, as Staz herself would have said, *verklempt*.

When we finally did recover, Geoff was the first to speak. "My mother is going to disown me when she finds out her first grandson is named after a pair of Catholic strangers."

Staz waved a dismissive hand at him. "Leave that part out. Tell her he's named after two of the most courageous people we've ever barely known."

Gene was shaking his head. "I don't know what to say."

I leaned closer to the tiny, sleepy bundle in my best friend's arms. "You can say hello to Nicolo Gail Greenfield-Molinsky."

CHAPTER EIGHTEEN
DON'T STOP BELIEVIN'

Five days and two funerals later, Mrs. Reale stood with me in the foyer of an auditorium labeled Wesley Hall. Seven Dolors Catholic Elementary School would not reopen in the fall. In response to parental concerns regarding the likelihood of toxins on campus, for these last few weeks of the semester, classes had been moved to the Religious Education Wing of the nearby Methodist church.

"How come nobody ever does anything to the Methodists?" Mrs. Reale muttered. "They're never in the news! Thank you so much for doing this for us, Mary Cath—I mean, Ms. Wheeler. The children will truly enjoy this, I just know it. Not that we have many left, of course. Even with just two weeks to go, over half of our families transferred to public schools. How are *you* feeling, anyway?"

"Me? Oh! The concussion seems to have passed, thanks."

"No, I meant from the car-carmist—the stuff that made Sister so sick."

"Carmustine?"

Mrs. Reale gave a shudder. "I heard it made your asthma come back."

"Only temporarily."

"Thank you, Jesus," Mrs. Reale said, pressing her hand flat over her heart.

How had she known about my encounters with the carmustine compound? I guess you have to have organized crime and Big Pharma on your side to keep a secret from the secretary of a Catholic elementary school.

I looked down the brightly lit hallway of this well-funded addition. The walls were fresh, eggshell white and completely devoid of art. The floors were tiled in soothing pastel shades of mauve and seafoam green. This was a far cry from the dark, hardwood halls of Seven Dolors, the walls encrusted with curling prints of saints, holy water fonts at each entry, crucifixes on each squeaky-hinged door. A college achievement test analogy formed in my mind: this place is to Seven Dolors as a hospital is to home. It was squeaky clean, but so much was missing.

The interim principal, a lay teacher who'd been dropped into the job, introduced me to the twenty or so students, grades four through eight, filling the aluminum folding chairs. This was the most dead audience I'd ever encountered. Usually school visits were characterized by children glad of a break, eager to play instead of work. These children just seemed beaten. Their mobster school janitor had been murdered. Their school building had been taken from them. Droves of their classmates had gone away. Only God knew how many of them had parents who were about to lose their jobs. I wondered if Turo's triplets had transferred, too.

I automatically looked to the back row, the oldest students in attendance. There were only five back there: three indifferent boys, one small girl with glasses and thin blond hair, and one stocky girl with beady brown eyes who looked so bored that the only thing that might enliven her day would be a good fight with someone.

It was a look I had seen before on a face I had seen before.

Then, having introduced me as a Seven Dolors graduate, the acting principal asked the question I always hate having asked while I'm in the room.

"Has anyone read any of the Alexander McSomething series?"

Ugh. No pressure. It automatically pits all the kids into two groups: Alex fans versus people who think Alex fans are weird. At first, all hands stayed down. After a second of smiling at them uncomfortably, I caught the short blond girl in the back looking around guiltily. Then she lifted just her fingers off of her lap. The familiar-looking girl sitting next to her saw this gesture and made a soft "pft," noise.

"Sienna," the teacher said in a warning voice.

"Whatever." Sienna turned so she was almost but not quite facing the wall.

I wanted to ask Sienna a question, but I held off. Instead I launched into my usual presentation, starting out by asking each of them to think of a conflict they experienced in their own lives.

The small girl raised her hand. I nodded for her to speak. "Will we be talking about it with anyone else here?"

Sienna made another "pft" noise. "What kind of problems you have? Picking what encyclopedia to memorize next?"

All three of the boys laughed. Sienna got a satisfied look on her face and stared me down, daring me to say something. I knew that look. I'd received it often twenty-five, thirty years before, back when I was too frightened to take such a dare. But once a girl has survived a gunfight, it's kind of hard for a junior higher—or much of anyone else, really—to intimidate her.

I sidled up to Sienna's end of the row and leaned right into her face. I saw her shoulders stiffen with my intrusion into her personal space, but she did not break our little staring contest.

"Sienna?"

"Yeah?"

"What's your last name, Sienna?"

"Maldorone."

"Your mom's name is Gina, isn't it?"

"Yeah. So?"

It's so nice to be right. "I went to Seven Dolors with your mom. Did you know that?"

"No."

And she wanted to make it clear to me that she didn't care, but the other students, including the girl with the glasses, turned wide eyes and open mouths onto the conversation.

"Sienna," I said, "you seem like a pretty confident young woman. Would you call yourself confident?"

"You mean, like, I have self-esteem and stuff?"

I glanced over at the small, bespectacled girl. Now she was looking down at her hands and focusing a great deal of attention on her peeling cuticles.

"Yes, Sienna. That's pretty much what I mean. 'Confident' means you're comfortable with being who you are."

"Then, yeah. I'm confident. Nobody stings—"

"—like the Queen Bee?"

Sienna gaped at me. The girl with glasses nearly let her chin hit her knees. The guys in their row let out hooting laughter. One of them swore then said, "She even knows your line!"

Out of the corner of my eye, I saw the acting principal move to stand just behind these students. I caught her expression: her arms were knotted in front of her chest, her brow was furrowed, and her eyes were wide. She was nervous. I gave her a reassuring smile as I walked away from Gina Maldorone's daughter.

"Confidence," I said to the whole room, returning to the front. "It's a great beginning, but it's not the end. Sometimes you can't even tell if it's real. Confidence, the real stuff, does not come from thinking you're better than other people. It doesn't come from being smarter, faster, better at sports, or—"

Here I looked at the other girl. "—better at school."

Nearly identical frowns crossed the faces of both Sienna Maldorone and her bespectacled classmate.

I smiled at them both. "Confidence doesn't come from what is easy. It comes from surviving what is hard. It comes from facing a conflict and letting it teach you, sharpen you, chip off all the stuff that makes you something less than what you're meant to be. It's okay to be who you are, because that's all Alexander McSomething does. But it's even better to become who you're meant to be, and that's something so great only God can imagine it."

I looked up at the acting principal. She was looking at me thoughtfully, as were all of the assembled students. I had not known that any of this would be coming out of me, especially that last part about God. I stole a second to ponder that, and suddenly my fingers itched in a way I knew but with a ferocity I never before had experienced in all my years as a writer.

I couldn't finish this workshop soon enough. I needed to go out, get a new laptop, and start writing. Finally, I had an idea for the next Alex book.

Alas, that's the way writer's block always works. Just when I want to ignore the world and write, write, write, the world has other plans for me. I still had to finish here, and in a few hours, I would be going to the Walkerville Regional High School athletic fields. It was the night of the "Go for Gloria!" benefit for my former classmate, Gloria Benevento. I could have skipped it, but I had asked Gene to meet me there. Now that we had survived the funerals of both Mr. Celli and his mother, it was high time that Gene and I had a talk.

Hours later, as the angle of the sunlight cried "late afternoon," I shielded my eyes against the glare with one hand and crossed the parking lot of my new hotel. It was a

Friday afternoon, long after check out and well before any weekend travelers might be rolling in to Walkerville, so I was the only soul visible in the parking lot. I was showered, my hair was straightened, my makeup was freshened, and I was already shaking, and I hadn't even made it to my car yet. It was time to go.

I had a lot to say to Gene. I even had scripted it in my head, between jotting notes for the first chapter of the next Alex book. I was now muttering under my breath the words that I knew I would need to say to him.

"I think we both need to be healthy, body and soul, before we...." I trailed off, listening to the click of my heels against the parking lot. "Gene, I would rather die than destroy you. I don't want to be the one who—"

Six feet from my car, I froze in my tracks. Tucked under the windshield wiper was a piece of beige stationery folded around the stem of a tall, red poppy.

I swayed on my feet. I looked around. Just me. With trembling fingers, I lifted the note and the flower. Even all these years after proofreading traded essays in Sister Thomas Marie's advanced English class, I could still recognize the handwriting of Rosa Trinaglia.

Here's what I wanted to tell you in the coffee shop: Get over yourself. You only ever saw the bullets, never the people firing them. There's a whole world around you beside the one inside your head.

I leaned against my car and reread Rosa's words. She was right: I never did see the people firing. I only saw myself getting hurt. Just like every character Rosa and I wrote, every real-life person has some motivation. Mr. Celli knew that. Mrs. Marcasian knew that. That's what made them love the unlovable. That's what made it possible for them to offer their lives for innocent Nicolo, for laboring Staz, even for worthless, selfish me.

Chris Vitale's motivation had been greed. Bobby Campobello's had been sick lust. Both would be going to trial. But Mr. Celli and Gene's mom? They were two very different people, but they shared a motivation: faith in something larger than themselves. Compassion had been the end and the beginning of their courage.

Motivation. A reason for action. Now it seemed Rosa and her tall, red poppy were asking me, "What is yours?"

I twirled the stem and watched the petals flutter softly. Whatever my motivation was, I would need a lot of it to get me through my upcoming conversation with Gene.

***

The previous day, when Gene had asked if I would be going to Gloria's benefit, I had told him to look for me in the bleachers. Nervous and distracted, I kept my sunglasses on and scanned the crowd. I wended my way through the high school parking lot, following the arrow emblazoned upon a "GO FOR GLORIA BENEFIT REGISTRATION" banner. Numerous pink and purple balloons were tied to the softball field fence. The PA system was playing music we would have heard at a CYO dance, circa 1987.

Between viewings, funerals, and the Seven Dolors visit today, I had gotten a general sense that the prevailing mood in Walkerville was one of anxiety mixed with validation. The community's trust in The Powers That Be, A. K. A. Christopher Vitale, was now destroyed, along with the backbone of the local economy. However, as people arrived at the softball field, I could see that, while greetings were subdued, they were lightened with voices that sounded relieved.

I wondered why that was, but it didn't take long for me to figure it out. Not all of them, but several people ahead of me in the registration line picked up purple t-shirts after paying their donations. I soon saw those shirts had the word "SURVIVOR" written on them. I pulled out my smartphone and searched the Web for "survivor purple." The resulting page was full of purple ribbon magnets and t-shirts, all for cancer survivors. There were a lot of purple t-shirts at this benefit. Out on the pitcher's mound, Gloria Benevento was wearing one. Rocco Cargione was wearing one, too.

I had strong suspicions that most other towns would have had fewer purple shirts. That's why HBC had picked Walkerville: to use us. Nobody was happy that jobs and schools were being lost, but nobody wants to be used, either.

"Mary Catherine?" A woman's voice interrupted my thoughts.

Startled, I turned and found Tina Donato and Pasquale Marchione standing behind me in line.

"Oh, hi," I said, letting them hug me. "Great to see you both. I'm sorry I didn't get a chance to talk to you at Mrs. Marcasian's funeral yesterday."

Pasquale waved off my apology. "Are you kidding? We're the ones who should apologize to you. We wanted to wait in that long line of people trying to thank you and Gene for standing up to Chris Vitale, but my wife's bladder couldn't hack it."

Tina slapped his arm. "Thanks, Wally. Love you, too."

He leaned down to peck her cheek, and she grinned.

The line moved forward. I asked, "Tina, you're not playing today, are you?"

Tina rubbed her belly and shook her head, her glossy black ringlets swaying. "I don't think so. I'm not in eighth grade anymore."

"Congratulations, by the way," I said. "You look fabulous. You really do have that pregnancy glow. When are you due?"

"Two months to go," Pasquale said, rubbing his wife's shoulder, "thanks to Gene."

Tina saw my expression and laughed. Pasquale blushed scarlet and blurted, "No! It's thanks to me, but we couldn't have done it without Gene."

"Honey," Tina said, "you're not doing us any favors. What he means is that we'd been trying for years. It wasn't until Pasquale saw Gene after Mass one time that we found out there was a way to get me healthy enough to get and stay pregnant. Gene's practice actually has more success than IVF."

Softly, I asked Tina, "Do you have endometriosis, too?"

Tina nodded. "I did, but with help from Gene's practice, I'm very confident it's gone."

I studied both Tina and Pasquale. "You go all the way out to Harrisburg to see Gene?"

Pasquale nodded. "And it's worth every drop of gas."

"Where's the Ham," barked a voice, "you checking in?"

The line had delivered me to the registration desk. I faced forward once more and found that the volunteer serving me was one Gina Maldorone. I couldn't help but gasp when I saw that Gina was clad in a purple "SURVIVOR" shirt.

She curled her lip at me. "What are you looking at?"

"Sorry, Gina. I just didn't know—you had cancer?"

She made a "hmph" sound. "Yeah, thyroid, senior year of high school. Made me miss prom and everything. You didn't know? How do you think I got these curves?"

Thyroid cancer, I thought, the treatment for which destroys the thyroid, which then causes weight gain. I reflected on my previous schadenfreude at Gina's adult figure, and I immediately felt like, as Staz would say, toilet paper.

"I'm so, so sorry, Gina," I said. "Really, you don't know how much."

Her shoulders stiffened a bit then she looked down. "What are you sorry for? You never did anything wrong." Then she leaned over and said to Tina and Pasquale, "Like, literally, she *never* did anything wrong. Am I right?"

"For real, though, Mary Catherine," Pasquale said. "You and Gene exposing HBC? You're like some kind of heroes now or something."

I shook my head. "I don't think so. Believe me, I've done far more wrong than I've done right."

That last part I said directly to Gina, who, for the first time in my years of knowing her, went speechless. The words of Rosa's note came back to me. I had been so worried about Gina's "bullets" that I had never considered that even the bully had her own battle to fight.

I was desperate to change the subject. "Anyway, has Gene checked in yet?"

The mood instantly changed. Gina, Tina and Pasquale exchanged knowing looks. Well, I thought to myself, if they were imagining that Gene and I were off to start our official couplehood, they were likely in for disappointment. That is, if I could get through my prepared speech with my resolve intact.

"Yeah," Gina answered, "about ten minutes ago."

I paid a donation, made my farewells, declined to put my name in for the "schoolyard pick" team selection scheduled to start in the next fifteen minutes, then made for the bleachers. Just as I was about to start climbing, though, my phone buzzed with a text: *Look by the sapling on the east side of the field.*

East? Didn't he remember that I was never all that great with directions? I faced the sun, turned away from it, then shaded my eyes, looking for a little tree. By the time I found him, he was already on his way toward me.

When he saw me, he moved toward me slowly, as if

each step still hurt, but at least he was on his feet again. His bruises were nearly faded, leaving him looking wan rather than beaten. The descending sunlight cut shadows on the angles of his face. He looked every inch the doctor in his clean khakis, pale green shirt, and a sport jacket. There were circles under his eyes, but he had shaved and otherwise looked well-kept.

Forget "well-kept." He looked amazing. I immediately berated myself for being so attracted to him, and I curled my fists. I was ready to have a fight with my own heart.

We stopped a yard apart from each other, each of us afraid of that moment where we don't know whether to shake hands or embrace.

"Hi," he said, leaning back onto his heels.

"Hi," I said. "How are you feeling?"

"Fine, all things considered. You look great."

Oh, Gene, please don't go breaking my resolve. "No, you look great."

He did not smile, but his eyes sparkled like I'd never seen. "How did this morning go?"

"Fine. Gene, I'm sorry, but I really need to talk right now."

Gene sighed through a tight throat. "I know. I have something I need you to know."

"But I have something I need you to know first."

Gene was reaching into his jacket pocket, and I heard his fingers brush briefly against paper, but he froze and put both hands in his pockets. "All right. You go first."

"I want to talk about that promise you made during the eighth grade retreat."

He startled slightly, his cheeks turning a faint pink. "What about it?"

My next question was going to be the most difficult for me to ask, the most difficult to hear answered. "Gene, do you—do you want to find out what we might be to each other?"

I was staring down at my fist resting at my side. I kept my eyes down because I did not want to see Gene's face, did not want to see in his eyes what answer he would give before he gave it. What I saw, though, was his hand moving to mine, opening the curl of my fingers so naturally. He pulled me toward him so slightly that I could not even call it pressure.

"I do," he said.

His thumb ran lightly over my knuckles, and I nearly caved. This time, he was the one reaching for me. This time, I had to be the wise one, the strong one. I was the one who pulled away.

"But see, I would rather die than destroy you."

Pain flooded his eyes. "What does that mean?"

I did not know I was crying until I drew my next breath. I flicked away my tears with the back of my free hand. "Gene, I love you because of your faithfulness, your truth. What you say, you mean. I can trust you like I've never trusted anyone before. I can trust you with my life. I can trust you with my soul."

He closed his eyes and shook his head in disbelief. "What about any of that makes you think that you of all people could ever destroy me?"

"Because you're still married, and it's not to me. If we are together before your annulment, you're being unfaithful, and I can't bear to be the one to take you down that road."

Gene was perfectly still for a perfect second, and then he laughed in a way I'd never heard before. "This is about my annulment?"

I nodded and squeezed my eyes shut. "Gene, you are strong and brave and generous. You are faithful beyond

anything I could ever dream of finding in a man, and I'm—
I'm not good enough for you. Okay, so I stopped taking
The Pill—"

"You stopped—?"

"—but I know that's not enough. You deserve so much
better than me and my weakness and self-centeredness."

While I spoke, he was lifting my hand, opening my fist
and placing my trembling hand between both of his. After I
stopped speaking, Gene just held my hand there between us.

When I remained silent, he said, "Mary Catherine, open
your eyes."

I did. I saw his left hand on top of mine. He wore
nothing on his ring finger but a tan line.

I turned wondering eyes to his. "But—?"

"You were right." He reached back into his jacket
pocket and pulled out a business-sized envelope. "It turns
out I did have grounds for an annulment."

He handed the envelope to me. I looked at him,
bewildered, then I looked at the envelope. The return
address read, "Archdiocese of Philadelphia Marriage
Tribunal."

I looked back up to him. He was smiling, his eyes
shining at me. "I'm free," he said.

My hand hung there, shaking, holding the letter. "But
am I? Why would you want me? You're so good, and I—
I'm just so fallen away."

He pulled me one step closer. I could feel both of our
hearts beating in our joined hands.

"Then let me catch you," he said.

I should have let him go, but I just couldn't. "Why
would you even want to?"

Again he laughed softly. "Why wouldn't I? You know
I'm not perfect either. And that promise I made at the
eighth grade retreat?"

I swallowed hard. "You kept it, you know. You made yourself someone's hero. You're mine."

He ducked his head, looking into my eyes. "I was making that promise for you, even then."

I snickered. "Sounds less like a promise, then, and more like a curse."

Gene shook his head. "It's not a curse," he said. "It's just chemistry."

We let our foreheads touch. Both of us let out nervous, laughing breaths.

"So," I said when I couldn't take the silence anymore, "what do we do now?"

He squeezed my hands. "You know the benefit of being the class outcasts?"

"We can cut out of here and nobody will miss us?"

Gene nodded. "Dinner?"

I giggled. "As long as it's not Chinese."

He pulled his head back, looking baffled. "Why not Chinese?"

I backed away from him so we could see each other more easily. "Remember the lab rat delivery system? What has been seen cannot be unseen."

"Ah." His laugh was now more relaxed. "Anyway, I think I still owe you some tomato pie."

"That sounds—"

Shouts reached us from across the fields. "There they are!" "Over there!" "Under the tree!" "Are they sitting in a tree?" Laughter followed. The PA system that had been playing 80s party music now blared with the voice of Rocco Cargione, "WILL MARY CATHERINE WHELIHAN AND EUGENE MARCASIAN PLEASE COME TO THE PITCHER'S MOUND."

Gene and I exchanged a confused look.

"HURRY IT UP, YOU TWO!" Rocco drawled into the

microphone, to uproarious, good-natured laughter from the gathered crowd.

Said crowd was collected around Gloria Benevento, standing atop the pitcher's mound, gesturing with one arm for us to come closer. Gene and I ran over there as quickly as we could. The crowd parted for us.

"What's up?" I asked Gloria, as she breathlessly reached out to hug me, then Gene.

Her thin face was gaining a healthy pink color, and her smile grew. "It's time to pick teams for the softball match. I want you both on mine."

Gene and I startled. "I don't understand," Gene said. "I didn't sign up to play. Did you, Mary Catherine?"

"Sorry, but I didn't," I said to Gloria. "I just came out to support you."

"But," Gloria said, "it's my benefit, and I want you both on my team."

I shook my head. "Why on earth would you want us? I don't know if you remember this, but neither of us could play when we were in school, and I don't know about you, Gene, but even if I had become an athlete over the past twenty-five years," I gestured down to my feet, "I'm wearing heels!"

For the first time ever, the whole crowd got my joke.

Gloria, however, was not laughing. She said, "Walkerville is a small town."

Jennifer Russo spoke up. "We've all heard by now what you did. You exposed what has hurt all of us."

Pasquale and Tina were there, too. Pasquale said to Gene, "Bro, you lost your mom, and you almost lost your own life, just to bring us the truth."

Tina looked to Gene, then to me. "You fought for us."

Even Gina Maldorone stepped forward. "You fought for all of us."

Gloria, with tears in her eyes, threw her arms around my shoulders then Gene's. "So of course I want you on my team!"

Gene was clearly too overcome to speak, clamping his mouth shut in order to remain master of his emotions. I, however, couldn't leave the intensity at such a high level.

I quipped, gesturing once more at my inappropriate footwear. "Are you sure? Are you that ready to lose?"

More laughter broke the tension. Again, Gloria did not laugh. "This fight isn't about who's the best pitcher, batter or fielder. If you two are on my side, we've already won."

Gene and I exchanged looks once more. He shrugged and took off his sport coat. "Tomato pie later?"

I leaned in and whispered just so he could hear. "Is that a promise?"

Epilogue
Peek-a-boo

Standing here in the shade didn't seem to be making a difference. He could feel the armpits of his t-shirt darkening with sweat. Summer was practically here. The sun was already throwing heat waves up from the softball field down the slope. He felt safe in this tree cover that edged the far end of the athletic zone of Walkerville High. He lifted his old binoculars to his eyes. After that, it didn't take him long to find her. He felt himself shiver in spite of the heat. It was like a fever, what that red hair of hers still did to him. After all these years, seeing her still made him sick.

Sick in a good way.

Seeing that tall guy with her, however—the doctor, they'd told him—made him sick in a bad way. It almost made him vomit, the self-control he needed to hold back from running the guy down and just cutting him then and there.

Faintly, he heard her name. Had she been right? Was he really going crazy? No. They had just called her name over the PA, that was all. They called the doctor's, too. She startled at the sound and tucked her hair behind her ear, hair redder than the edges of a campfire. Once he'd had that hair wrapped up in his own fist. He'd let her slip away. He'd let her threats, another man's threats, and police with their stupid harassment reports stand between them. If she had just given him one more chance, he could have explained himself. He could have won her back. He would have won her back.

How could this doctor call himself a man and not be kissing her right now, to have her that close?

Two days ago, two men had found him. He had just been out on lunch break, alone as usual, when these two dudes came up.

"Sean Chambers?"

He'd put down his beer. "Yeah?"

"Sean Chambers who's on file with the police for having harassed one Mary Catherine Whelihan?"

His throat went dry. He wet it with his beer before nodding. "That was in the '90s."

"Would you like to get her back?"

His answer was quicker than a heartbeat. "Yes."

He'd expected mob guys to wear suits and dark glasses. These wore khakis and golf shirts. One was even blond. It didn't matter what they looked like, though. They were going to help him, they said. The only price he had to pay was patience.

Through his binoculars, he watched her smile. He smiled back.

END

AUTHOR'S NOTES

In spite of all our current medical knowledge, both the causes of and the most effective treatments for endometriosis remain a mystery. *Don't You Forget About Me* is a work of fiction, and as such, scientific research can spark the author's imagination. This is a work of fiction, and all medical and scientific conjectures imagined herein are just that—imagined.

When it comes to facts, there are treatments available for women's health issues that do not involve hormonal birth control. Some sources for more information about these approaches:

- Natural Procreative Technology: www.naprotechnology.com
- Couple to Couple League: www.ccli.org
- One More Soul: **www.onemoresoul.com** (This site also has more information about the documented dangers of hormonal birth control.)

ACKNOWLEDGEMENTS

My heart overflows with thanks both for the grace of God and for all the good people He has put in my life.

First, I must thank the Catholic Writers Guild in general. In particular, Joseph Cabadas of CWG got the Tharsis Tuus critique group started, and he was the first from that group to give me feedback on early drafts of this manuscript. Ann Margaret Lewis called me one spring morning and encouraged me to try the Guild's online conference. Because of Ann's prompting, I put my doubts aside and later found myself in a chat room with Ellen Gable Hrkach of Full Quiver Publishing. One year later, I am thankful that Ellen is the Mary Poppins of editors—kind but firm, and generous with the spoonsful of sugar. Meanwhile, AnnMarie Creedon has combined the roles of both mentor and cheerleader, and in the short time I've known her, she's already become my "sistah from another mistah." Last but hardly least of the CWG crew, Margaret Realy has been a blessing to me on so many levels that I could write a whole book about *that*.

My dear, dear friend Nada Wanner was the first to read early drafts of this story with excitement, and her excitement has long been the candle to light me through many dark times; our texting habits perhaps leave Mary Catherine's and Staz's in the dust.

I am also deeply grateful to my army of social media friends who cheered me on every time I posted the next chapter title. Deserving of special shout-outs are PJ Cabrera and Glenna Heckler-Todt who stepped in with suggestions when I had hit various walls.

Any mistakes in this novel are completely my fault and not due to any neglect or disinformation on the parts of the following four people who answered my calls for help.

Patricia Katzenmoyer, CRNP, and Helen LaFrance, PA, FCP, got me on the right track for much of the medical research needed in the writing of this story. Jennifer McNulty Breen answered my questions about pharmacology in a most helpful way. I also must thank Robert Motley, MD, both for giving me necessary details about current research and practices in Catholic women's health care, as well as for being brave enough to chaperone that dreadful "Bandfest" fundraiser when I was the youth minister at his parish back in the '90s. That he answered the phone when I called years later is a testament to his generosity.

To my fellow Little Flower moms (V. G., M. I., N. K., C. C. D.), your friendship and support mean more to me than I could ever express.

I am also grateful for the serendipity that allowed Kamila Zrebiec to be resuscitating her own artistic dreams at the same time as I was; her multidimensional empathy has been a true gift.

I cannot forget my Dominican family, especially J. Catherine Sherman, O.P., for showing me that writing is an apostolate and for introducing me to the fullness offered to the laity in St. Dominic's embrace.

I would be remiss were I not to thank the Ambler Catholic Elementary School Class of 1987. I learned a lot from you then, and I continue to do so.

I must also give a special thanks to my children for helping Mommy write by staying (mostly) quiet during Quiet Time, for learning how to wash dishes and sort laundry, and for eating a lot of meals out of the microwave with little to no complaining.

Lastly, I must thank Scott, who after fifteen years of marriage still loves me enough to get jealous of fictional men and who still takes my breath away.

Requiescat in Pace — *Hãy An Nghỉ*
Tung M. Huynh
ACES '87

About the Author

Erin McCole Cupp is a wife, mother, and lay Dominican. She has written for *Canticle Magazine*, *The Catholic Standard and Times, Parents*, *The Philadelphia City Paper*, and the newsletter of her children's playgroup. Her first novel, *Jane_E, Friendless Orphan: A Memoir* is available on Amazon. Readers can connect with Erin on her website at erinmccolecupp.com.

48464818R00121

Made in the USA
Charleston, SC
03 November 2015